FOR *You* HAVE SINNED

CLIFFORD EDWARDS

Print ISBN: 978-1-54399-740-8

eBook ISBN: 978-1-54399-741-5

THIS BOOK IS DEDICATED TO Yoli, for her faith, to Jen, for her patience, and to Mitch, for his inspiration.

Also for Ralph, who let me stay in his basement in Washington.

Damian Alexander, when someone says you're not good enough, don't give them the satisfaction of being right.

You are better than you know.

"Thou shalt not bow down thyself unto them, nor serve them: for I the Lord thy God am a jealous God, visiting the iniquity of the fathers upon the children unto the third and fourth generation of them that hate me,"

-Deuteronomy. 5:9 KJV

> **"Then when lust hath conceived, it bringeth forth sin: and sin, when it is finished, bringeth forth death."**
>
> -James 1:15 KJV

HIS TONGUE WAS GONE. HE was fairly certain. A metallic scent, like old copper pennies, burned through his nostrils. He tried to cry for help, but his lips were sealed, glued together with what must have been blood. He gurgled viscous bubbles in the back of his throat as he searched for his voice. A small chunk of shredded flesh, playfully, flicked at the rear of his vacant mouth like an artist's paintbrush. The intense pain kept him teetering on the brink of sanity. Where, in God's name, am I? A warm trickle of liquid coated the exposed flesh of his inner thighs. It was as if he was pissing himself, but from the excruciating agony in his groin, he was convinced, that would never be possible again.

From his limited vantage point, he could tell he was in a cavernous, poorly lit room. The light from a single torch attached to a limestone wall made it possible for the shadow demons to carry on their whimsical dance. The air was heavy and the room was silent, except for the occasional drip of water and the sound of his own labored breathing. His ankles, legs, wrists, and arms were bound, keeping him affixed to the shoddy linens that separated him from the stone slab upon which he lay. Though his head was free to move, the soreness in his throat and face, along with the precarious nature of the situation, made him apprehensive to twitch a muscle.

However, if there were any chance for survival, he needed to scrutinize his surroundings for any possible way out.

He mustered up the strength to move his head to better assess his situation. He painfully flexed his neck muscles and twisted his head to the right. An endless hallway led to blackness and the darkened entryways of several passages that were barely visible beyond the edges of the firelight's weak glow. The old bones in his neck cracked as he attempted to swivel his head to the left. Through his peripheral vision, he could just make out the outline of a metal table, similar to one found in an operating room. He strained to get a better look.

On the side table, was a device that appeared to be scissors of some sort lying next to a set of green shears with jagged blades resembling the head of a crocodile. Both, sat in small pools of coagulating blood. Next to the instruments, were two lumps of severed flesh. One was considerably longer than the other. As he processed his situation, he heard the sound of stone grating on stone, as if a heavy door was slowly sliding open. Footsteps descending a staircase could be heard in the direction just beyond his feet. Terror overtook him, and he slipped into darkness.

He woke up suddenly to find a creature ripping apart the tender flesh of his bottom lip. As his good eye adjusted to the grisly scene, he was almost relieved to find a grey cat licking at the dried blood around his mouth. Though each swipe of its sandpaper tongue felt like a punch to the face, he calmed and dreamily smirked while processing the utter absurdity of his predicament. This was followed by a cough combined with a bubbling wheeze. The feline, displeased by the reaction, turned around to focus on more interesting matters. The cat's tail brushed against his nose like a curious cobra. He had always considered cats to be assholes, and now, adding insult to injury, he found his face just inches from both.

There was a strange feeling in his stomach; or was it on his stomach? He felt the claws of the cat on his chest, yet there was a similar sensation on the skin of his abdomen. Could there be two cats? This felt different. He tried to look down his body but, still, only saw the posterior of the grey cat.

He sensed movement in the far corner of the room. Something had changed. He wasn't alone. He fought against his restraints with what little strength he had left. Startled, the cat quickly relocated to the small metal side table to his left.

His eyes widened with horror. Just past his feet, he saw a hooded figure working diligently over an open flame. Then, his strong eye focused on the curious scene before him. On his stomach, rested a glass box. The box had a lid with a small round metal knob screwed into the top and it lacked a bottom panel. Inside the box, were two large rats; one black, one white. He could feel their clawed feet prick at the skin of his belly as they took in their new environment, looking for an escape. The cat watched hungrily from his perch atop the metal side table. What have I done to deserve this?

The cat was gingerly sniffing at the lumps of flesh on the table when the hooded man approached steadily, with purpose. He was wearing a black leather mask and tightly gripped a wooden shaft. A steel plate fixed to the top was glowing so red hot, the wooden handle was beginning to smolder. The plate was similar in size and shape to the lid of the box. He was at the foot of the stone slab in seconds. He said nothing, and removed the glass lid.

The prisoner jerked violently against his restraints to no avail. How could this be happening? Why has God forsaken me? His hooded captor was at his feet, wielding the heated metal like a plunger, and through the holes in his mask, stared intently into his eyes.

He recognized those eyes! A lifetime of harsh memories streaked through his mind like a bullet train. He came close to smiling as the man in the black leather mask applied the heated metal to the glass box on his stomach.

The rats scrambled frantically as the metal plate closed in on them. They desperately needed a way out, and their only way was down. The large rodents clawed and chewed through the flesh of the man on the slab. Blood splashed against the walls of the glass box as the rats ripped through fat and muscle and began working on the visceral layers of membrane covering his intestines.

His executioner never broke eye contact. The dying man could feel the world slipping away. He no longer experienced pain, nor fear. He had come to terms with what he had done and why he was here. As darkness closed in, he saw the grey cat jump down and disappear into the shadows, the larger chunk of flesh from the side table dangled from its jaws. In his frenzied delirium, he was laughing hysterically. He really didn't have anything left to say.

1

EL PASO, TEXAS
September, 1988

SHE COULDN'T HELP BUT SMILE, as the cool morning wind lapped at the soles of her bare feet hanging outside the passenger side window. It was the first taste of autumn after a blistering Texas summer. Temperatures would probably reach the 90's by next weekend, but nothing was going to spoil this glorious Sunday. Everything was perfect.

Lupe gazed lovingly at the amber slopes of the Franklin Mountains just beyond her toes. She couldn't recall a day when they looked more majestic and serene. Visitors would scoff to hear the locals refer to them as "mountains". As a young girl, she had taken a bus from Seattle to Ellensburg to visit some second cousins. She knew what mountains were supposed to look like, but these would do just fine.

They continued west on I-10. Just to the south, Lupe saw the vibrant colors of laundered garments pinned to clotheslines, swirling in the wind like an unbridled ballet folklórico. Children kicked a soccer ball between makeshift goal posts. She could almost hear them cheering each other on with each pass. The day was just beginning, and already promised to be unforgettable.

El Paso would always be home. She was born and raised here. Her friends liked to call it, "El Chuco". She never understood that. It was supposed to have something to do with a Mexican gangster style zoot suit fashion craze from the 30's, but she also knew "chuco" to mean "filthy". There was nothing filthy about El Paso, especially, when you were in love.

Lupe glanced over to the driver's seat. There he was. She studied the outline of his face, dusky and perfectly angled, long black eyelashes hypnotizing her with every blink. Joe kept his eyes on the road. It was early and they hadn't spoken much, but there were no awkward silences. Berino, New Mexico was less than a half an hour away. Joe felt Lupe's stare and reached out his right hand to pat her thigh reassuringly. He turned and smiled at her before returning his focus to the highway. For a second, she was lost in his beautiful, big, brown eyes.

Joe was an apprentice mechanic at his Uncle Guillermo's garage in East El Paso. He'd spent the last six months working extra hours to provide as much assistance as he could toward Lupe's nursing school tuition. She graduated in July, but they both knew it would be a long time before they could get everything paid off. She was working part time in the children's ward at Providence Hospital, picking up as many hours as the administration would allow. The young couple understood they would have to spend many hours apart to be together, but they had a wedding to plan for and, at least, they had Sundays.

The engine of Joe's 1973 Chevy Nova purred as they crossed the state line into New Mexico. The car was definitely a fixer upper but it was Joe's project and his passion and Lupe loved being in the passenger seat next to him. The original green-gold metallic paint was barely visible through the grey primer and Bondo, but Joe's dream car "ran good" just as the ad had promised. Joe recently replaced the interior with the seats from a totaled Chevy he found at the "Pick n Pull" next to his uncle's shop. The car was his pride and joy, next to Lupe, of course. She made it look good no matter how many dents and scratches were on the outside. If they only had more money, they'd be cruising in style.

They would be arriving at their destination a little earlier than planned. There was no traffic on the road and with a population around 1000, Berino was no booming metropolis. Neither of them had spoken a word which was unusual, but not alarming. Lupe looked over at Joe and noticed a look of concern on his face. She felt it was time to break the silence.

"You look very handsome today, mi cielo," Lupe began, "After the service today, I'm going to make whatever you want for dinner, even that stinky stuff your mama makes with the cabbage and the cheese that smells like feet. I'll wear that dress my tia made. It's pretty short, baby. I can't wait to spend tonight with you. Is every thing ok? You look like you're worried about something."

"It'll be alright, Lupita," Joe said. "Remember that money I borrowed from the reverend the last time he was in town?."

"Yes," Lupe answered. "I put the last of it in the jar when I got paid on Friday. Did you forget the jar? It was all there. I counted it on Friday."

"I didn't forget the jar, baby," Joe said. "I needed something for the car to make sure we could get here today. I borrowed a little from the jar yesterday. We're 54 dollars short. Hopefully, he just lets us work it off today. I hate not having money! I'm sorry baby."

"Don't worry Joe," Lupe reassured. "The reverend is a reasonable man. He was nice enough to give you the money in the first place. He'll understand. He's a man of God. I'm sure he'll understand."

"Thanks Lupita," Joe said as he smiled at her. "You're the best, baby. Lets go make some money! By the way, everything you make smells like feet and I have a feeling you won't be wearing that dress for too long tonight." He put on his left blinker, "I love you."

They laughed together as they pulled into the dirt parking lot. A huge black and white striped tent flapped in the morning breeze, waving them in. A banner over the entrance read, "Welcome to Brother Buddy Kind's Holy Rolling Revival!" It was time to pay the piper.

* * *

"SOPHIE, REMEMBER TO KEEP THE cripples and the retards in the back this time, for Christ's sake! You know I can't do shit for them. We don't want another incident like in Terlingua last week. That old bastard cost me 75 bucks to reset his nose and another 50 to keep it out of the paper. Naldo, you're in charge of the temps. Get some to clean up, some collecting donations, and some selling lemonade. If you see any stealing, I want them removed immediately. I want their names, where they live. We're making dreams come true here, people! Big smiles. Folks are going to start arriving soon. Lets be ready this time. Sophie, cue the choir just before I come on. I want them singing. This is a revival damn it!"

When the Reverend Brother Buddy Kind spoke, people listened. His indisputable charisma and natural good looks made women melt and men take notice. He was a slim 6 foot 3 with a strong build, perfectly white smile, and piercing blue eyes. Not a single blonde hair was out of place. He kept it combed back to prevent any distraction from his sculpted face. He spoke with a thick East Texas drawl that dripped from his lips like honey. Buddy Kind could charm the skin off a rattlesnake.

Naldo Ortiz was Buddy's right hand man, and not just because his left hand was mangled in a hay baler six years ago at the age of 14, leaving him with a withered claw. When Buddy found him, he was peso-less; unable to find steady work because of his disfigurement, and living on the streets of Juárez. Naldo always thought of Buddy as his savior and his Savior. Naldo was the only person Buddy truly trusted. He was the biggest Mexican he had ever seen. Naldo was best suited for security, but he was willing to take on anything Buddy required of him.

It was about an hour until showtime and Buddy retreated to his dressing room in the back of one of the two construction trailers behind the tent. Sophie greeted the guests that were trickling in. She had them fill out prayer cards and meticulously took note of where she sat them, marking their seat numbers at the top of the card. She would make sure Buddy was privy to this information prior to cue-ing the choir. Everything was in place and going smoothly.

Buddy relished the time he spent alone just before the show. He prepared himself mentally, occasionally checking the many mirrors surrounding him for stray eyebrow hairs or tooth debris. He snacked on a pastrami sandwich and a garlic pickle that Sophie brought to him before the pre-show meeting. Sustenance was essential. The people wanted a spectacle and he was going to give it to them, hard. He pulled open one of the metal filing cabinet drawers and reached into a container marked "Grand Finale". Buddy placed a red capsule in both of the pockets of his white jacket. Now he was ready.

* * *

JOE AND LUPE GOT OUT of the car. They had to park at the far end of the temporary dirt lot even though there was ample parking closer to the venue. It was part of the Employment Agreement. The Holy Rolling Revival only passed through Berino a few times a year but they were no strangers to the rules. It was easy money and they never missed a chance to spend some time together and see just what Brother Buddy Kind would get up to next.

They held hands during their long walk to the show tent. A shiny new black Cadillac Brougham was parked in the spot closest to the entrance. The vanity plates read "B Kind" and Lupe giggled as Joe rolled his eyes mockingly. Sophie greeted them at the entrance with a smile. "Hi ya'll", she said, "Back for more punishment, huh? You know where the uniforms are. Get suited up and meet me back here. I think we'll have Lupe on refreshments today and Joe, you can be on cleanup."

"Thanks Sophie," they said in unison and marched their way behind the wooden stage to collect their work clothes. There was a rolling metal clothing rack with shirts hanging on wire hangers. They looked for their sizes and put them on. They were unflattering grey bowling shirts with "Holy Rolling Revival" embroidered in large neon colored letters on the back. On the front it read, "Next to Godliness Crew".They grabbed blank badges out of a plastic basket and pulled markers from an old coffee can sitting on a small table and wrote in their names. Joe grabbed a broom and dustpan, Lupe grabbed a hand truck, two water jugs filled with lemonade, and three sleeves of plastic cups. They reported back to Sophie.

Sophie checked them off the list and they made their way to their respective stations, Lupe, behind a rickety table and Joe, trying to look busy amid the sea of folding chairs. Seating was almost at capacity. Hopeful congregants waited eagerly for their prayers to be answered. Six black women in white choir robes walked in, single file, to their positions on the set of bleachers next to the stage. Four people in wheelchairs were craning their necks at the back of the crowd. Joe looked over to Lupe serving lemonade. She winked and blew him a kiss.

* * *

BUDDY LOOKED AWAY FROM THE mirror in front of him when he heard the music start. The choir began clapping and singing. He wasn't sure of the song but there were plenty of "Hallelujah's" and that was most important. He rose from his chair, did one final check of his smile, straightened his tie, and made his way out of the trailer. He stood behind the white curtain, waiting for his cue.

A quick burst of light was followed by trails of smoke from the budget pyrotechnics in place on either side of the stage. Nine doves were released into the air. Usually, ten took flight, but, sadly, there was one more incident in Terlingua last week. The Reverend Brother Buddy Kind took the stage and the crowd went wild.

Like the rest of the audience, Joe and Lupe could barely take their eyes away from the man in white. For nearly two hours, Brother Buddy Kind commanded the audience with his theatrics, prayers, and titillating anecdotes. A morbidly obese man with diabetes was more than convinced his insulin levels were under control. An acne riddled teenager in a "Bangles" concert shirt finally realized he was being punished for his impure thoughts and not his hormones or poor hygiene. A woman with arthritis in both knees threw down her walker and hobbled quickly from one side of the arena to the other while hiding the pain from the audience, and herself. The choir sang and the people rejoiced. Brother Buddy's work was almost done.

"Friends," Buddy preached, " I just want ya'll to know that I love each and every one of you. More importantly, Jesus loves you. Some of the members of our family will be passing around offering plates. Remember, the greater the seed you sow, the more you will reap the fruits of salvation. Please, dig deep into those pockets." The reverend put his hands in his own jacket pockets to drive home the point, as well as collect the two essential items for his climactic culmination. "Bow your heads and pray the Lord's prayer with me."

Buddy's sermon ended with a resounding "Amen". The people looked up to find their prophet standing on the stage, eyes closed, arms outstretched with open hands. Blood dripped down the center of each of his palms. He fell back into the arms of two crew members conveniently waiting on stage to catch him. The reverend was dragged off stage through the curtains. Three women fainted in the front row.

There wasn't too much to clean up after Brother Buddy's performance. Just a few plastic cups and used tissues that were strewn about the grounds. Joe helped Lupe move the water jugs back to where they belonged before assisting the other "grey shirts" with folding and stacking the chairs. There was a different team that would take down the tent, probably the same one that put it up. It was almost time to pick up their checks but Joe was apprehensive to approach Buddy with the story of his insufficient funds. He and Lupe remained at the back of the line to avoid a scene with too many onlookers.

As the last of the temporary workers made their way out of the trailer, Joe and Lupe pushed in. Buddy was sitting at a desk, hovering over a checkbook with pen in hand. Naldo loomed ominously behind him. After seeing who had come through the door, Buddy said, "Well, look what the cat drug in. Hey, Joe. I believe we have a little financial matter to discuss before I go handing out checks. You do remember that, right Joe?" Joe felt a droplet of sweat make its journey from his temple to the bottom of his cheek.

"About that, sir," Joe stammered, "I'm a little short, but I thought maybe you could take it out of this check and if there was anything unpaid, you could take it out the next time you came into town. I had to make some repairs on my car and it was either that or..."

"You must not understand how this works," Buddy interrupted. "We had a deal. I loaned you some money with the promise that you would give it back to me, in full, today. Was I not clear about that when we made this arrangement, Joe?"

"Sir," Lupe chimed in, "you can take all of my pay today. I'm sure that will more than cover it. We are so sorry. Things have been tight, with bills and..."

"Joe," Buddy said, raising his voice. "Kindly, tell your lady friend that grown folks is talking. There's going to be some paperwork to fill out and I really hate paperwork."

"I'm really so sorry for the inconvenience, sir," Joe apologized. "We had all of the money on Friday, but things just, happened. I won't let this ever happen again. We love working here. It was a great sermon today. Really inspiring."

"Naldo," Buddy said, "Im going to need you to take Joe here, next door to fill out some paper work. Can you do that for me?" Naldo walked over to Joe then looked back to his boss. Buddy gave Naldo a nod and a quick wink.

Lupe started to follow Joe and Naldo out the doorway when Buddy stopped her. "It's just going to take a minute, honey. Take a load off. Let's sit a spell." He guided her back to a chair and locked the door.

* * *

LUPE HEARD AN UNSETTLING COMMOTION coming from next door. She could feel the vibrations through the floor as if furniture were being thrown around in the adjacent trailer. The first scream was the loudest, followed by quiet whimpers, and then silence. She ran to the door to unlock it but the large hand around her throat made any escape attempt, futile. Buddy was right behind her, pressed up against her back, and whispering in her ear.

"You know what I like about 'Mescan' women?" Buddy misspoke intentionally. "It's their loyalty, but most of all their passion." The scent of rancid deli meat and garlic made her gag. His hot breath burned the back of her neck and she began to cry. "That man of yours is going to pay his debt today. You can be sure of that. I don't take kindly to being screwed over. He's going to pay his debt and you, little lady, are going to do your part to save his life." He reached around her waist and popped open the button on the front of her pants. Lupe's watery eyes stared blankly at nothing. She was numb.

Lupe sped through the shit stained, barren wasteland to Las Cruces. It was about the same distance from Berino as El Paso, and nobody at the hospital would know her. Joe regained consciousness several hours after he was admitted into the ER. She was able to clean up most of the blood from Joe's new upholstery, especially the stains she'd left on the driver's seat. She always kept an extra outfit in the trunk. She had to change her pants and discard the evidence. She prayed that Joe would never notice. She prayed about so many things. She prayed more that day than she ever would again.

* * *

FRISCO, TEXAS

"GOOD MORNING FATHER DANIEL," THE children chimed harmoniously. He had officially been a priest for just over a year and Daniel still had not quite grown accustomed to being called "Father". At 29, he was pretty young for a priest but he graduated from The University of Dallas with a 4.0 GPA and went on to ace his seminary courses, finishing early. He found it easy to focus on his studies without the distraction of a social life. Father Daniel never cared much for the casual company of others, except children. Children were pure and innocent, unfettered by the evils of the modern world, at least while they were young. As Deacon, Daniel was able to lead a youth catechism group before mass on Sundays and he was grateful he was still able to sit in during Mrs. Fischer's class.

Edna Fischer sat quietly at her desk while Father Daniel addressed her pupils. She began volunteering at the church after her husband died 4 years ago. She was a short, round woman, equal in height and width. Her cherubic face was replete with laugh-lines and her nose and cheeks, with gin blossoms, revealing her determination to pursue happiness, by any means necessary. Like the seams of her green polyester pantsuit, she dealt with stress with the utmost tenacity and fortitude. Mrs. Fischer was pleased to let Father Daniel speak.

"Good morning children," Father Daniel replied. "I hope everyone is well. Before I let Mrs. Fischer get back to teaching, I just want to let you know how happy I am you all made it again this Sunday. There will be mass right after class so make sure you take care of all your socializing now. You must remain quiet during mass. I'm sure Mrs. Fischer has some great activities for you today. Remember, Jesus loves you."

The youth group consisted mostly of the parishioners' children, though some of them were bussed in from an orphanage in Oak Cliff, about thirty minutes away. Father Daniel liked to begin his few minutes with a couple of songs and then open up for questions and concerns. He had a mass to get mentally prepared for. He didn't have much time, but he relished every second with the children.

Father Daniel noticed a child in the back of the class wasn't joining in. Daniel knew him as Luke. Luke's attendance to their weekly gathering was sporadic. Today, Luke sat silent, his right arm in a sling.

"What has happened to you this time, Luke?", Father Daniel inquired. Last month, he noticed Luke had two black eyes and a bandage on his forehead.

Surprised to be called upon, Luke muttered, "I fell down at baseball practice again."

"I think you may need to try another sport, son," Father Daniel advised. "Baseball doesn't seem to be agreeing with you."

A precocious seven year old named Emma was quick to raise her hand. "My step mom says that God in the Old Testament was mean," she exclaimed, "He killed people for no reason and I shouldn't pay attention to that God. Why is the old God so mean?"

Not expecting an inquisition, Father Daniel was notably unsettled. "Sometimes," he stammered, "we don't always understand what's best for us. Fortunately, God knows what's best for us. Your parents may tell you not to do something that you really want to do because they know what's best for you. They want to protect you, and God wants to protect you. God is like a parent who knows what's best. Mrs. Fischer, I have to get ready for mass. Thank you children." Father Daniel left the room.

Mrs. Fischer made her way to the front of the classroom. "Children, get out your crayons. We're going to color Moses parting the Red Sea. Remember, the sea isn't red, right kids? This is going to be fun!".

Luke did his best not to go outside the lines. He wasn't used to coloring with his left hand.

* * *

FATHER DANIEL OPENED THE HEAVY door to the rectory to find Father Quinn dozing off in a chair. It was a familiar scene of late, and he walked quietly to avoid startling the slumbering priest. Daniel stepped over to the small kitchen, which was only inches from the living room, and began heating a kettle for tea. A closed door to the back of the room led to their chamber. They shared a bedroom; two twin beds separated by a night stand and a lamp. These were modest accommodations to say the least, but they required no more than the simplest creature comforts. Their close quarters allowed Daniel to take better care of Father Quinn and set the stage for enlightening conversation.

The whistling from the kettle roused Father Quinn from his midmorning nap. Though a bit groggy, Father Quinn seemed delighted to have company, and company serving tea, was better yet. As the son of Irish immigrants, he was partial to his morning tea; and the occasional afternoon whiskey. Father Quinn rubbed the sleep from his tired eyes, yawned, and smacked his lips before finally speaking.

"Daniel, is that you, my boy?", Quinn inquired. His weakening eyesight made it difficult to see much more than blurry shapes without his glasses. With his glasses, he could see marginally better and he was less likely to remove an eye with his teaspoon.

"Yes Father," Daniel replied. "I'm sorry to wake you, but I thought you might like some tea."

"No apologies are needed when there is tea involved. How was Mrs. Fischer's class this morning? All bright and bushy tailed, I assume. My hat's off to the woman. It's hard to keep a child's attention for more than a few seconds nowadays unless you're dressed like a yellow chipmunk or something. I can't seem to break them away from their telephones for five minutes. So it was a good morning so far, son?"

Daniel couldn't hide his smile. Hearing the old man reference a Japanese video game craze, tickled him. Father Quinn was 81, but his wits were as sharp as any of his classmates from the seminary. Daniel saw him as a real father and, more importantly, a true friend. The tea was ready. Daniel placed Father Quinn's cup on the table in front of him, three sugars and lots of milk, just the way he liked it.

"It was a pleasant morning, as usual, Father," Daniel answered. "We sang and prayed together. I left Mrs. Fischer a little early so she could get to some of her art projects. I did have a question from a new girl named Emma, that took me a little off guard."

"And what was that, son?" Father Quinn felt around for his cup on the table and Daniel pushed it closer until his fingers touched the handle.

"She said her step mom told her the God of the Old Testament was bad. She thought we should ignore that part of the Bible and wanted to know how God could be so mean. I didn't want to say anything she might not be ready for, so I stumbled a bit and left the room."

Father Quinn put on his glasses and stirred his tea before speaking. "It's a wonder parents even bring their children to church anymore, always trying to undermine us at home. How can we set the foundation if they keep breaking it?" The old priest brought the cup of tea to his lips and, with an audible "clink", hit the rim of his bifocals with the spoon handle. "Daniel, the Bible is full of parables and allegories. It's full of metaphors. It may be unpopular in some circles, but through my years, I've learned to take the meaning of scripture with a grain of salt. Otherwise, we'd all be waiting outside the Red Lobster with a bag of rocks. Let's save that for the fundamentalists", he joked. "The Old Testament, and much of the Bible, is about being accountable for our actions. For a child, it can be as simple as Santa Claus not bringing you presents for acting out in school. Focus on the message without giving nightmares. I've always told you, my son, punishment comes in many forms, but it is a necessary good. I guess what I'm saying is, people, even children, must know there will always be consequences."

As Father Daniel absorbed the words of his mentor, there was a knock at the door. When Daniel answered, he was greeted by Sister Sarah, a young nun, volunteering from an abbey in Fort Worth. Despite her petite stature, her voice echoed in the empty hallway. "There is a scheduled confession in 10 minutes," she informed.

"Be a dear and take this one, will you?", Father Quinn asked Father Daniel. "I'm not sure I can pry myself off this seat."

Father Quinn hadn't heard a confession in over a year. Daniel knew his place and was happy to oblige. "I'll be there in five, Sister," Daniel said. "Thanks for the reminder."

* * *

HE WAITED IN SILENCE IN the confines of the ornate oak confessional for at least 15 minutes. Confession was one of the duties of the priesthood that Father Daniel enjoyed the least. Listening to people drone on about their virtuous shortcomings, only to absolve them of guilt, seemed a bit counterproductive. Where was the accountability?

The door on the other side of the booth finally opened and a man knelt down in front of the latticed screen. Father Daniel kept his eyes forward, patiently giving the penitent time to collect his thoughts. In his peripheral, Daniel could almost make out the pattern of the man's blue and white shirt. The stale scent of last night's overindulgences wafted through the partition as the man began to speak.

"Forgive me Father, for I have sinned," the man started. "This is my first confession. Sorry, I'm not really sure how this is supposed to go. My wife said I should do this. It was either this or counseling. She says I need to get some support or she'll make things real shitty for me. Sorry Father, I mean, … stinky? It could get bad for me." Every utterance wreaked of insincerity. He spoke softly with a nasally twang. "She says I can be mean," he continued. "I don't intend to be. I never been mean to her. I promise. Her son comes here. I dropped him off a couple hours ago. I'm sorry for all this stuff. Please let me be good in the future. Amen."

Father Daniel sat in quiet contemplation. He had to do what he'd never done before. "It's imperative you find peace in your life and the lives you impact," he finally instructed. "You most likely need more assistance than I am able to offer. Therefore, I am unable to grant you absolution. Start by coming to mass today and, hopefully, I will hear about your resolutions in next week's confessional. Please schedule with Sister Sarah before you leave today."

"You serious?" the man questioned. "I gotta do this again? I gotta get here next Sunday and tell you what you wanna hear?"

"Until next Sunday."

"Is there someone else I can talk to?"

Silence.

"Alright, thanks for nothing, man. Laters."

* * *

WITH HIS SCHEDULED CONFESSION CUT short, Father Daniel was able to walk the grounds of the church and take in the day, before starting mass. Saint Anthony Of Padua Catholic Church was an unassuming rock structure off Farm to Market Road 423, near Panther Creek, just north of downtown Frisco. It was a short commute to civilization, but from where Father Daniel was standing, it could have been a thousand miles.

Daniel walked past the gates of the small cemetery at the back of the church. He spent many of his days here during seminary, tending to the grounds and earning his keep. Some of the headstones dated back to the late 1800's, and though he had each one memorized, rereading the indented inscriptions brought to him an inexplicable serenity. As money was always tight at the church, Father Daniel was still in charge of the cemetery. He wouldn't want it any other way.

It was almost time for mass. Father Daniel stopped at the statue of Saint Anthony in the courtyard. He looked into the eyes of the baby Jesus, held lovingly in Saint Anthony's arms. Daniel grasped the crucifix from around his neck and brought it to his lips. He kissed it and said a prayer. People were starting to arrive. He was ready for mass.

On his way to the church, Father Daniel noticed a commotion in the parking lot. Standing among the arriving cars was a tall, thin man in an overly starched plaid blue and white shirt and jeans, roughly ushering a child into the cab of his black Chevy truck. With his arm in a sling, the young boy could do little to protest. There would be two more empty seats at mass today.

* * *

"ROLL UP THE WINDOW, MIJA," Lupe's mama said from the front passenger seat. "It's too windy in here."

"I like the way the wind feels on my face, and it's my birthday so I can do what I want."

"Not until Tuesday, Lupe. No special treatment until Tuesday. Are you excited to go camping, mija?"

"We go to Big Bend every year for my birthday," Lupe replied. "It is beautiful, though. Yes mama, I am excited."

"It's tradition," Lupe's papa chimed in from the driver's seat. "You don't mess with tradition."

"At least this year you have your own tent," Lupe's mama said. "You're moving up in the world. I can't believe you'll be 18 next week. Where does the time go? I remember when I could hold you in a blanket around the campfire, and when you caught your first fish and it jumped out of your hands. You cried so much when we threw it back in the river because you wanted to take it home and keep it for a pet. We're so proud of you, Lupe."

"I love you, mama." Lupe patted her mother's shoulder from the backseat.

"We love you too, mija," her parents said together.

Lupe grabbed the crank on her right and rolled her window up an inch, feigning compliance. She breathed in the warm air as it caressed her cheeks and playfully ruffled her long black hair. Across the vast sea of cacti and desert succulents, she could just make out the shape of the Chisos Mountains on the horizon. Lupe smiled. Then, the sky turned dark red.

Puzzled by the sudden change, Lupe called out from the back seat, "What happened to the sky? What's going on?"

Ominous black clouds rolled in ferociously, covering a red fiery sky. Her mother and father said nothing as they continued to speed toward the bridge ahead. "What's happening, mama?" Lupe screamed. "Papa, what happened to the sky?" Her parents were silent. "Why won't you answer me?" The car accelerated. The entrance to the long, two lane river crossing was only yards away. Everything was happening so fast. "Please answer me! What is happening?" Lupe could hear the low growl from a huge truck engine up ahead in the distance. A black, semi-trailer truck drove onto the bridge from the other side, and stopped. Two dark blasts of smoke erupted from the exhaust stacks, and the engine revved

In desperation, Lupe removed her seat belt, slid over to the middle, and pushed her head into the front seat. Her parents' faces were frozen in terror. Their bulging, bloodshot eyeballs stared blankly from lidless sockets. She tried to shake them, but they were strapped in tightly to their seats by at least a dozen seat belts; wrapped around their chests and arms and covering their gaping mouths. The car continued to speed onto the bridge. The black truck jerked forward and started its approach from the opposite side. The gap between the two vehicles closed quickly, though the bridge appeared impossibly long.

Time stopped, then started again slowly. Lupe screamed, "Papa, watch out for the truck!" They were, now, only a few feet from the chrome grill of the oncoming semi. Lupe peered through the windshield of the18 wheeler. Sitting in the cab, was a man in a white suit with slicked back blonde hair. He was staring back at her from behind the steering wheel. He smiled openly, exposing several rows of sharp teeth. An unnaturally long forked tongue wagged from his toothy maw. His wide yellow eyes fixated on Lupe. The interior of the cab appeared to be engulfed in flames. It was the Reverend Buddy Kind.

Lupe squeezed her eyes shut and raised her hands to cover her ears as the semi struck the front driver's side bumper, sending the 1978 Ford Fairmont station wagon into a violent spin. Time sped up. Lupe was thrown against the inside of the door. Her head slammed against the window frame. She could hear several ribs cracking as her body collided with the armrest and window crank. The sounds of shattering glass and squealing tires were drowned out by her own screams. Her parents remained silent.

Lupe was pressed up against her door while the station wagon spun out of control. The scenery sped by in a blur outside her window. Then her neck whipped to the side like a rag doll as the car came to an abrupt stop. The front end of the car had burst through the steel guardrail. The station wagon teetered on the edge of the bridge. Only the twisted metal of the mangled guardrail digging into the back end of the wagon kept the car from falling into the ravine. Lupe needed to act quickly.

"Mama, Papa, are you alright? Can you hear me? Please answer me!" From her position in the back seat, she tried her best to pull at the many seat belts that wrapped around her parent's torsos, but they were bound tightly and Lupe couldn't find a single release to unbuckle them. Suddenly, the station wagon lurched forward. Like nails on a chalkboard, the guardrail tore into the sides of the car as it staggered further over the edge. Looking out of the windshield, Lupe could see the river water below.

She needed to find something to cut the straps, fast. She dug through her purse and found a nail file. She didn't have time for that. She found a small rectangular mirror. The edges weren't sharp enough to cut through anything, but she decided she had to make it work somehow. Lupe tried to bend the mirror in her hands, but she wasn't strong enough. She frantically searched for something to break it. She pulled up the silver door lock knob and slammed the mirror onto it. After several attempts, the mirror shattered. Lupe looked at her bloody hands and found one sharp piece of glass she could use. A massive engine revved in the distance. When she looked out of her window, Lupe could see the black truck was stopped at the other end of the bridge. The truck's bright reverse lights cut through the darkness.

With no time to waste, Lupe began sawing at her mother's restraints with the shard of broken mirror. She was more successful cutting through the flesh of her palm than the polyester webbing of the belt, though it didn't diminish her efforts. Lupe almost fell into the front seat as the station wagon dropped a few more feet over the edge of the bridge. The reverse lights of the semi were rapidly approaching.

Lupe felt a brief moment of satisfaction when a seat belt snapped in two. She looked up from her handiwork and turned her head to look out the window. The rear end of the black truck was only centimeters away. It smashed into the back of the station wagon and the guardrail released its grip. The station wagon began its descent to the river below.

When the front end of the car hit the water, Lupe was thrown into the front seat. Her forehead slammed into the dashboard. The car hesitated for a moment after impact, then flipped over completely. Water began pouring in through the floorboards and Lupe's open window. Lupe turned herself around and sat dazed on the ceiling of the Ford Fairmont, staring into the bloated, purple, upside-down faces of her parents. They appeared to have been dead for days rather than seconds. Water was closing in all around her. She was ready to give in to the river.

As the water reached the bottom of her nostrils, Lupe suddenly found the strength and will to survive. She inhaled one last deep breath and pushed her way past the lifeless bodies of her parents, through the open back passenger side window. She gasped for air when she finally surfaced. She swam as fast as she could to the nearest bank of the river and reached it just in time to see the tires of the family station wagon disappear under the water. She climbed onto a rock to catch her breath. Lupe coughed up water, then began to cry.

Lupe's sobs were interrupted by the howl of a wild animal. She turned her gaze toward the sound. Looming on the bridge between the shredded guardrails, was a creature that Lupe could not identify. She blinked and tried to refocus. She could barely make out the silhouette of a giant beast standing on two legs. From her vantage point, the thing appeared to have the haunches and curled horns of a mountain goat. A tuft of blonde hair on the top of its head blew in the wind. Her mind was surely playing tricks. It was dark. She shook her head and looked again. It seemed to be holding a tiny animal with a long thin tail, above its head. Lupe could only stare in disbelief.

Lightning flashed and Lupe was able see everything clearly for a brief moment. The thing on the bridge was staring at her with yellow eyes and a wide toothy smile. She could barely make out the crucifix around its neck as it glinted in the flash of the lightning strike. It was holding a human baby between two cloven hooves; a bloody umbilical cord dangled from the infant's belly.

Lupe instinctively reached for her stomach. It was round, but felt hollow. Lightning struck again. Lupe looked down to see her thighs were coated in blood.

2

EL PASO

June, 1989

LUPE WAS JOLTED TO CONSCIOUSNESS; her hands held her pregnant stomach. She put one hand between her thighs and brought it in front of her face. She was relieved to see that there was no blood on her fingers. She hadn't had a good night's sleep in months, and last night was no exception. The nightmares were becoming more frequent. She decided to keep them from Joe. She kept a lot of things from Joe during his recovery. Lupe lay on her side, awake, sweating, and staring at the wall. The pillow between Lupe's legs offered nothing more than a distraction from the soreness of the chafing on her, now, more than ample inner thighs. The cramps in her stomach were worsening. For weeks, Lupe had been suffering from bouts of diarrhea, and she had no plans to sully her clean floral sheets, again.

Lupe needed to get to the bathroom across the hall in a hurry. She swung her heavy legs from the sheets like a pendulum, losing the thigh pillow in the process. She painfully propped her body up onto her right elbow and stopped for a brief respite before returning to her, nearly, insurmountable journey. Lupe gasped and grunted before finally managing to get upright and sitting on the bed. The next part would be harder still.

On wobbly legs, she was finally standing, one hand on the bedpost for stability, the other pressed firmly on her aching lower back. Like a little teapot, she took her first step toward the bedroom door. Lupe opened it and waddled into the hallway. The smell of boiling beans and sizzling bacon from Joe's mother's kitchen made her instantly nauseous. She couldn't wait for this to be over so she could, once again, enthusiastically stomach the delicious breakfast tacos Joe's mama made.

Lupe peered at herself in the bathroom mirror. Her young face looked haggard. Her swollen belly had dropped since last night. From her nursing training and the few lamaze classes she and Joe actually attended, Lupe knew the phenomenon to be called "lightening", or the descent of her uterus into her pelvic cavity. The cramps were getting worse. She had some unfinished business with the toilet and carefully lowered herself onto the seat.

A sharp pain shot through her body as her abdomen tightened up. She winced in pain and gritted her teeth. She felt a glob ooze from her, and into the bowl. Given its consistency and origin, she didn't need a nursing degree to know this wasn't loose stool. Her mucous plug had, well, unplugged.

"Joe!" she screamed with tears streaming from her eyes. "I think it's happening! It's happening, Baby! I need you!"

He only had a few finishing touches to add to the baby's room. Joe had spent the last few weeks preparing for their new arrival; painting his parent's spare room yellow since Lupe had not wanted to know the sex of the baby. Yellow seemed like a neutral enough color. The crib he made from some scrap lumber he found at some odd jobs was just about finished. Fortunately, Joe was as handy with a hammer as he was with a wrench. He made sure everything was sanded down and baby proofed.

Lupe didn't have much family. In fact, he'd never actually met any of her relatives. Joe heard her talk about some relatives in Washington state, but he'd never met any of them. Her mother and father were killed in a car crash when she was seventeen and she'd been on her own when Joe first met her. Lupe was resilient. It was one the qualities he admired most in her. That, and her loyalty and devotion. She was his rock, especially during his recovery. The last year had been very trying for them both, and she never left his side.

It just made sense for them to move in with his parents. Joe's parents had the space and he and Lupe were still struggling with bills. It was nice to have family to depend on. Joe was trying to save up money for a ring and a modest wedding, but, life happens. At least he still had Lupe. She didn't want to look pregnant in the wedding photos, anyway.

He could smell breakfast cooking from the kitchen. All this baby proofing was making him hungry. He found a stopping point and mopped his brow.

Suddenly, Joe heard Lupe screaming from down the hall. He jumped up and started running toward her. It was time!

* * *

JOE REACHED THE BATHROOM IN seconds flat. He saw Lupe sitting naked and crying on the toilet. He helped her to her feet, wrapping her in his old plaid robe he found bunched up on the floor. He escorted her down the hall and through the door leading to the garage.

Joe's mom was quick to turn off the burners on the stove. She grabbed the duffle bag next to the sofa in the living room, as they had rehearsed, and made her way to the car. She opened the back passenger side door and quickly got in.

Joe made sure Lupe was secure with safety belt and blanket. He had placed towels over the upholstery in preparation for this moment. He ran around the car and jumped in the driver's seat.

Joe quickly exited his Chevy Nova and ran into the kitchen. He grabbed the car keys off the wooden key rack attached to the wall and bolted out to the garage. He stopped short, and ran back into the house to find his shoes.

He finally turned the key in the ignition and they were speeding down the drive on their way to Providence Hospital.

Lupe's water broke minutes before arriving at the ER.

* * *

JOE PACED BACK AND FORTH between the rows of seats in the waiting room. His mother sat quietly knitting the tiny yellow socks she had started a few days earlier. Sweat was dripping from Joe's temples. He was anxious and excited.

A few hours had passed with no word. Lupe didn't want anyone in the delivery room and Joe was fine with that, given his aversion to blood and his recent phobia for hospitals. He just needed to know she was alright and that his baby was healthy.

Joe's dad finally arrived. He'd managed to get out a little early from the nearby racetrack where he managed a small janitorial crew. Joe had his family surrounding him. All he needed now was some good news from the doctor. He couldn't wait to hold his baby. He longed to hold Lupe and kiss her on the forehead.

It was at least two hours more before the doctor emerged from Lupe's room.

"Everything went extremely well. You can go see your new baby, Joe," the doctor said. "Lupe's waiting for you."

Joe was giddy with nervous excitement. He trembled from head to toe as he made his way to the doorway of the hospital room. Joe peeked around the corner at the two people he loved most in this world. Lupe appeared to be resting. She held a blanket wrapped bundle on her chest. Joe approached the bed.

"Hey baby", Lupe murmured as she pried open her eyes. "I love you." Her words were muddled by the drugs and exhaustion. "Hold your baby, baby," she giggled as she slurred.

Joe carefully picked up his son. His baby's eyes opened just long enough to meet Joe's loving gaze. "I love…," Joe began to say, but stopped short. He hesitated, suddenly unsettled. He stroked his son's head, combing back the few wisps of blonde hair growing on the baby's pale head.

Joe immediately returned the baby to Lupe's chest.

"Pinche puta!" Joe exclaimed.

Lupe held her son close. Through tired half open eyes, she watched Joe storm out of the delivery room. It was the last time she would ever see him.

* * *

FORT WORTH, TEXAS

"GET A LOAD OF THAT fat fuck," Tony said, as a spotty faced, wild haired teen in a faded, extra small concert shirt walked out of the convenient store across the street. They watched him from the unmarked grey Honda Civic, as he sauntered past the barred windows of the store. He precariously held three tall energy drinks in his arms, intending to consume at a later time. The open bag of pork rinds would not be so lucky.

"I bet he doesn't know shit about Pink Floyd," Tony said. "These kids with their video games and they're posting every goddamned thing on the internet. They got nothing to say and they never shut the hell up, am I right, Aaron?".

Detective Aaron Rider usually enjoyed his partner's banter, but they were going on 11 hours together today on this particular stakeout, and his patience was starting to wear thin. They had talked about everything from French cheese to new math and Aaron would have liked nothing more than a bit of silence.

"You know what I really miss? Good spaghetti," Detective Anthony Donolla answered himself without giving Aaron a fighting chance. "Ma's spaghetti. Shit here's like ramen noodles and tomato juice." His words were heavily sauced with the influence of every mob movie from the last 50 years.

Tony was a beat cop from Upstate, New York. He transferred to Texas from Rochester a little over a decade ago, but from the way he spoke, you would think he had grown up in Brooklyn in the 1930's. He had planned to move up the ladder to homicide detective in a "real city", but not one quite as "real" as New York, so he and his wife headed down to Dallas. His wife thought Texas was a wholesome place to start a family. 10 years and 40 pounds later, and it was still just him and her, but from the things he'd witnessed on the job, he was more than convinced that was a good thing.

They sat in silence for a while. Although, Tony could talk a blue streak, his conversations were usually one sided and required only the occasional grunt to keep him satisfied. Aaron had plenty on his mind and was relieved to have had Tony as "background noise", but he also relished the quiet. They were confined to that tiny car in that shitty part of downtown Fort Worth for a reason. They had a job to do.

Less than two weeks ago, Arthur Riggs came home to his public housing project apartment off Rosedale Street, to find his girlfriend paying a debt to her dealer with more "personal" means than money. Riggs stormed into the other room to alleviate his concerns with a volatile combination of crystal meth and PCP. When the noises from the other room subsided, Riggs confronted his partner's infidelity. The next day, two children discovered a human ear in the rusty playground on the property and reported it to the police. After breaking down the door of number six, the officers found a headless woman in the living room and a head in the freezer. The coroner found traces of Arthur Riggs' semen in and around the vacant left eye socket and a few strands of red pubic hair frozen to the cheek. The eyeball was never recovered.

The detectives were parked outside a known drug house in Southeast Fort Worth. Riggs had been known to frequent the residence, and as junkies rarely put too much effort into branching out of their comfort zones, the two cops felt they were probably barking up the right tree. It was day three, and it was really taking it's toll on their collective mental soundness.

Tony broke the brief silence. "Hey man, how's your wife doing? I don't like to ask, 'cause I know it's a sensitive topic, but I do care, you know? How's Scottie holding up? Hey, how are you doing buddy?"

"About the same," Aaron said, wishing he didn't have to have this conversation again. "Scott's still torn up. He's with the babysitter now. It's hard to talk to him without getting too emotional. I don't want him to see that. I'm doing alright, I guess. It's hard, though. Life'll throw you some curveballs."

Aaron hoped that was enough of a response to change the subject. His wife, Heather, was diagnosed with a brain tumor a few weeks ago and she fell into a coma soon after. He didn't know much about her condition, other than it was very risky to operate in her current state. He tried to visit her in the hospital when he could, but it just hurt more. He kept his son, Scott, away as much as possible, but he had so many questions and missed his mom.

"You know, I go to that big church thing on Sundays with my wife. She makes me go, but the guy puts on a show. Shit, never a dull moment. Pastor Jacob Dwyer or Dreyer or somethin'. You should come with. Bring Scottie. Maybe, it'll make him feel a little better. You could do with a little Jesus, you miserable fuck."

Aaron appreciated Tony's effort at lightening the mood. He didn't have the heart to let Tony know that he had given up on God since his wife's diagnosis, and, realistically, long before that. Aaron offered a crooked grin and nodded his head. "Yeah, maybe."

Tony saw that he may have struck an uncomfortable chord and decided to change the subject. "You see what these girls are wearing these days? I seen this girl, must have been 16, with her dad, no less, ass cheeks hanging out her shorts like they was rationing denim. Personally, I'm glad I got no kids. No offense, but seems like a lotta' trouble nowadays. How am I not supposed to look? World's turned upside down."

"It's crazy, for sure."

A man in a black hoodie walked up the pathway to the house across the street. He carefully surveyed his surroundings. A shock of auburn hair blew in the breeze from beneath his hood.

* * *

"DISPATCH, UNIT 814 REQUESTING A 10-13, East Lancaster and Lumber. We're going to need backup, quick," Aaron said calmly into his lapel mounted two-way radio. For the last two days, the detectives had little else to do but study old mugshots and family photos of Arthur Riggs. Certain their man had arrived, they would wait for backup and take the perp down, hopefully, without incident.

"Riggs, put your hands on your head and get down on the ground! Now!" Tony screamed from outside the car with his Glock 22 in firing position. Apparently, the rules had changed.

Detective Rider was forced to spring into action. He wished he'd been better prepared, but the academy had taught him to think on his feet. He feverishly fumbled for the door release and jumped out of the car, joining his partner, firearm drawn.

The man in the black hoodie looked up and flashed a smile like Indian corn. He winked just before bursting through the door of the dilapidated house. The door slammed shut behind him. It was "go time"!

The detectives approached the house quickly and cautiously. This wasn't how it was supposed to go down. Aaron could hear sirens in the distance, but they weren't nearly close enough to prevent whatever "shit show" they were walking into. The two cops arrived at the door, stood on opposite sides of the jamb, nodded to each other and tested the knob. Locked. Tony took a step back and kicked in the door.

"Police! Get on the ground! Let me see your hands! Get on the ground! Now! Don't move, you piece of shit! Hands where I can see them!" Tony demanded, breathing heavily. Three men sat, bewildered, on a stained couch in the middle of the room. With bloodshot eyes, mouths open, and hands in the air, the men seemed too frightened to follow any further instructions. A dark haired woman lay face down next to an overflowing cat litter box. The stench of marijuana smoke, urine, and cat feces was unbearable, despite the efforts of the burning incense coming from the golden Buddha statue next to the digital scale on the cracked glass coffee table. In Buddha's arms was a bowl of tightly wound plastic baggies containing small white rocks. Twenty dollar bills were stacked haphazardly on the table. The man in the black hoodie was nowhere to be found.

"Where is he? Where'd he go? Answer me!" Aaron pressed. The man sitting in the middle of the couch cocked his head to the side, motioned with his eyes, and lowered one hand just enough to point down the hall. At that moment, the sound of breaking glass came from a room at the back of the house. "Cover them, I got it."

Aaron moved expeditiously down the hallway. He arrived at a door, slightly ajar, and stopped for a second to assess the situation. He could hear whimpering from the other side. He pushed the door open and found Arthur Riggs' legs dangling from the small broken bathroom window. Blood spilled down the wall onto the floor. Aaron grabbed the back of the black hoodie and pulled Arthur Riggs to the linoleum. "You're under arrest, asshole." Aaron put his two-way radio close to his mouth. "Dispatch, 814, we need a 10-52." Paramedics would be sent to remove the 9 inch piece of glass from Arthur Riggs' abdomen. As the color faded from Arthur's face, Aaron proceeded with the Miranda warning. New voices could be heard from the front room. Backup had arrived.

* * *

THREE MEN WERE ESCORTED OUT of the house in hand-cuffs. Arthur Riggs and an unidentified woman were taken out on stretchers by the paramedics. There would be so much paperwork to follow. In the commotion, Detective Anthony Donolla was able to pocket a small stack of twenties and a few plastic offerings from the bowl of the golden Buddha. There was more than enough evidence to go around.

3

DALLAS, TEXAS

June, 1995

"COME ON MIJO, STAY CLOSE baby," Lupe said. "We have to keep moving, Chuy. Other people need to get off too." She held her son's hand tightly and stepped off the bus and onto the tarmac. A wall of heat and exhaust fumes welcomed them to Dallas. Anyone who recommends travel by bus, has never gone 12 hours through Texas in mid June, with a six year old. Lupe was so grateful to get off that bus.

They weaved through the crowded terminal, and onto the street. Lupe could feel the stares, but she had grown accustomed to it now. It must seem strange to some people to see a dark skinned, Hispanic woman leading a little blonde, blue eyed child by the hand on this side of town. If it was in a nicer neighborhood, she may have been confused for his nanny.

Lupe pulled a small piece of paper out of her pocket. She jotted some directions down before they left El Paso. Only six blocks to the Weary Traveler Motel. The motel boasted free cable television and air conditioning. At this point, Lupe only cared about the latter. They weren't here for a vacation, and at $19 a night she would happily forgo any other amenities. She needed a shower to wash off the last 12 hours, then she could begin to think about what she came here to do.

Life had been hard on Lupe the last six years. She couldn't imagine her life without Chuy, but the sacrifices she made had been tough. She had to start working part time at the hospital and could only afford a small efficiency apartment in East El Paso. After groceries, day care, rent, and bills there was little left at the end of the month for anything else. She would have left Chuy back home if she had any family or friends to look after him. Reparations were long overdue.

They hurried past several sleeping figures occupying the doorways of abandoned buildings on their way to the motel. Chuy hid behind his mother when panhandlers approached for spare change. She shooed them away without making eye contact. Her neighborhood in El Paso wasn't much different but at least, there, she knew the lay of the land.

Sweat beaded on Lupe's brow and she wiped it off with her sleeve just before opening the rickety door to the office. A red neon sign that read "ACANCY" flickered in the window. A pair of rusty metal bells jingled above their heads. The office was empty.

On the counter was a chrome call bell and a handwritten note reading, "Ring Bell For Service". Lupe pushed it once and waited, then pushed it again. Two minutes and many rings later, a short, round Indian man approached the counter from the back office.

"Okay already, I'm hearing you. I'm coming, I'm coming'" the man said in a thick Indian accent. Lupe looked down at Chuy and winked. They shared a smile while she stroked the back of his head.

"How can I help you Miss?" the clerk asked.

"Hi sir, we called ahead. I'm looking to get three nights with a queen size bed for me and my son."

"You and your son, okay." The slight pauses between the words gave Lupe the impression the clerk wasn't buying the whole situation, but with the dingy outdated decor and less than picturesque location, she was certain the Weary Traveler Motel had seen more than its fair share of questionable weary travelers.

"Yes, three nights and I'd like to pay in cash up front." Lupe

"It is $65.12, please. Check out is at 10:30. Your room is number 7 on the first floor facing the parking lot. The ice machine on your floor is not working but there is one on the second floor on the opposite side of the building. Please be enjoying your stay."

"Thank you," Lupe said, exchanging the money for a room key attached to a blue plastic key ring with the number "7" written on it in magic marker.

Lupe and Chuy walked across the parking lot to their room. They passed two men in white tank tops sitting in the bed of an old Chevy pickup, drinking 40 ounce bottles of beer wrapped in brown paper sacks. The men stopped their conversation to eye

Lupe up and down as she passed. They didn't even seem to notice Chuy was by her side. She smiled to herself. Still got it, she mused.

The key turned easily in the lock at number 7. They pushed their way inside. A musty air-conditioned draft blew Lupe's bangs away from her forehead and felt better than anything she could remember. The room was exactly how she pictured it. A queen size bed draped in a green and pink flowered spread was the centerpiece. Two framed canvasses displaying splashes of red paint were bolted to the wall, looking more like crime scenes than the intended abstract art. The bathroom countertop was branded with the marks of forgotten cigarettes, but the water came out hot and fast. For all intents and purposes, it was perfect.

Lupe took a long, hot shower, bathed Chuy, and dressed him in his dinosaur pajamas. She double checked the door and engaged the extra chain. They both climbed into bed and nestled beneath the covers. Lupe turned off the light and they were sound asleep seconds after their heads touched the pillows. It was just as well, Lupe had a big day tomorrow, possibly the biggest day of Chuy's life.

* * *

THE SCREAMS OF AN ANGRY woman outside the motel room woke Lupe from a deep sleep. "Take your no good, cheatin' bitch ass and get the hell outta here!" the woman continued. A man murmured something indecipherable and the woman proceeded with the tongue lashing. A bottle crashed into the pavement of the parking lot. "That's right, baby! Keep walking! Go back to yo little tramp. Broke ass piece of shit." It wasn't the wake up call that Lupe would have chosen, but she was up now and she had things to accomplish. Chuy slept through the whole ordeal.

Lupe turned on the lamp that was screwed into the nightstand by her side of the bed. She opened the drawer, pushed aside the bible, and reached for the yellow pages. She flipped to the "C'"s and found "churches", running her finger down the list until she arrived at "Reverend Kind's Christian Experience". She took a deep breath before dialing.

Chuy was starting to stir so she gave him his walkman and told him to listen to his music for a bit while mommy took care of a few things. This was not a conversation he needed to hear. He looked quite happy listening to some childhood classics and playing with his plastic Tyrannosaurus Rex. Lupe picked up the phone and dialed.

"Reverend Kind's Christian Experience," a vaguely familiar voice said. "This is Sophie. How can I help you?" Lupe was relieved to hear the friendly cadence of her old supervisor's words. It was Sophie from the salvation show.

"Hi, Sophie. This is Lupe Verdugo, I'm not sure if you remember me, but we used to work together every now and then when the revival traveled to Berino, New Mexico."

"Oh my goodness, Sugar," Sophie said. "I was wondering what happened to ya'll. How is," Sophie paused, "was it Joseph? Ya'll used to make my day."

"It was Joe, Sophie. We parted ways a while back. I guess it wasn't meant to be. I'm looking to get a hold of the Reverend. Is he there?"

"So sorry to hear that, Hun," Sophie said, sincerely. "The Reverend is here, but he's busy at the moment. Can I get a number or take a message for him?"

Lupe gave Sophie the telephone number at the hotel and told her she was in room 7. Now, all she could do was wait. She took the headphones off of Chuy's ears and turned on the television. They shared some snacks she had brought with them, and waited.

A few frustrating hours passed, and Lupe decided to call again. She reached Sophie and briefly explained how it was imperative she spoke with him today. Sophie cordially agreed to pass on the message, and the waiting resumed.

Six hours later, Lupe decided she had given up on "cordial". They were getting hungry and she was tired of the runaround. She would call in one last message.

"Sophie, just let the Reverend know I've been calling. Sorry, I don't give a crap if he wants to hear from me, but he might want to know his son has been asking about him. I'll visit, in person, tomorrow." Lupe hung up the phone.

* * *

"WHAT WE NEED, NALDO, IS some crazy shit. Get a few people on the staff to dance around like they was insane and full of the Holy Spirit. Scream some gibberish, you know, get the crowd goin'. I'll lay my hands on them like I'm going to inject the Spirit directly into them. They need to fall flat on the floor, and I mean fall like they ain't worried about hittin' their heads. We'll have people there to catch 'em. When they hit the floor, they need to sizzle like bacon;

like there was an electric fence under them. The rest'll follow. Trust me. Sheep man, we need sheep. And none of this dollar shit. We need to up the ante. Start at 20 bucks. We got bills now, rent. We need to start a Bible study on Wednesdays. Maybe a women's meeting on Tuesday or Saturday. We'll figure that out soon enough. Get people in the door, they won't be disappointed."

Naldo Ortiz efficiently scribbled the reverend's words into a notebook. The Buddy Kind Ministry had just purchased an old bingo hall a few months ago and they needed to make sure they had a viable business plan in place. They were located in a strip mall between a sandwich shop and a video rental store. The sign reading "Reverend Kind's Christian Experience" arrived two weeks ago. It was now proudly displayed over a black canvas awning that separated the glass windowed storefront from the roof.

"We'll continue with the ads but let's pull back on the interviews," Buddy continued. "No more call in radio shows. We need some folks putting fliers on cars, Sundays at the nearby churches. Let's do something for charity, maybe with a dog shelter or the," before he could finish, there was a knock on the office door.

"Come in," Buddy said. Sophie gently pushed open the door. "Reverend, there have been a few messages for you today," Sophie said.

"We're kind of busy here, Honey," the reverend explained. "I told you, just write them down. I'll look at them later."

"This one might need more immediate attention," Sophie said. "Do you remember Lupe Verdugo? Back in New Mexico a few years ago, she and her boyfriend, Joe, used to help with the revivals. Does that sound familiar?"

"We had a lot of folks work for us. If she wants a job, tell her to fax us a resume."

"Sir," Sophie continued, "She apparently needs to speak with you." Sophie said, now lowering her voice. "She says your son is asking about you and she's coming here tomorrow to talk."

"Hmm. Thanks Sophie," Buddy said, "leave me her number and I'll get in touch with her. Thanks so much." Buddy motioned with his head in the direction of the door. Sophie put the hand written message on the desk and backed out of the room.

The door clicked shut. "Naldo, I got a lot on my plate at the moment," the reverend said, "Im gonna need you to take care of this one."

Naldo nodded and left the room. He called the phone number Sophie left for them. "Thank you for calling the Weary Traveler Motel. Can I help you?"

"That's everything I need, thanks," Naldo said and hung up the phone.

∗ ∗ ∗

TODAY DIDN'T GO QUITE AS planned, but Lupe figured it was at least a step in the right direction. Tomorrow, she would accomplish what she came here to do. She was certain Sophie had passed on the message, if only the last one, and the reverend was probably mulling over his options. She didn't want him to be a part of Chuy's life, but she needed assistance. Child support would be ideal, however a generous lump sum of "hush money" would suffice. Lupe now held all the cards. No up and coming holy man wants a scandal.

Lupe was proud of herself. She had come to Dallas with a plan and it was starting to unfold. She hated the thought of blackmail and was terrified to have to come face to face with her attacker, but she had endured enough. It was time to get her life back.

It had been an exhausting day of waiting. They never left the motel room for fear of missing a call. Lupe was famished and she knew the crackers and fruit roll ups she had packed for Chuy were not enough to keep her son fed. He was a growing boy, after all. She had set aside a bit of extra cash for meals. Not wanting to take her son out into the night on this particular side of town, Lupe felt it was best to order in. She thumbed through the open yellow pages to "pizza", found the cheapest place that would deliver, and dialed the number.

They lay on the bed and watched some television. It was so nice to finally relax. The food was on its way. The lady at the pizza place told Lupe to expect a delivery in about 30 to 40 minutes. 20 minutes after placing their order, there was a knock at the door. "Mijo, go wash up for dinner," Lupe said. "Get under your nails. How did you get so filthy, baby? We didn't even go anywhere. You amaze me, Chuy." Chuy hopped off the bed, went into the bathroom and closed the door. She was pleased to hear the water running as she went to answer the knock.

She started to open the door but forgot that the top chain was still engaged. She pushed the door closed again to create some slack. "Just one second," Lupe said.

Before she could undo the chain, the door violently swung inward. Lupe was thumped in the forehead and lurched backwards as a broken link of gold chain flew into the room. A giant man in black, grasping tightly to a severed electrical cord, burst through the door, uninvited.

Lupe twisted and fell face first to the floor. Naldo straddled her body and wrapped the cord around her neck and pulled. He lifted her off the ground. Her feet dangled inches from the soiled olive green carpet. He closed his eyes and whispered a prayer behind her.

"Requiem aeternam dona ei, Domine. Et lux perpetua luceat ei. Requiescat in pace. Amen."

Satisfied she had lost consciousness, Naldo stopped pulling. With his left claw on top of Lupe's head and his right hand on the bottom of her chin, Naldo twisted with a quick jerk, cracking her neck in two places.

Lupe's body went limp and slumped to the floor like a discarded marionette. Eyes bulged out of a dark purple face. A crooked misshapen neck hung unnaturally to one side.

Pleased with his work, Naldo inhaled deeply and opened his eyes. A young blue eyed boy stood before him, tears welling in his eyes. Chuy's plastic dinosaur dropped to the floor.

* * *

NALDO LOOKED INTO THE REAR view mirror only to see the boy's big blue eyes staring back at him. His hands and feet were tied with electrical cord and he was strapped in tightly with the seatbelt. His face was expressionless and he made no effort to fight his constraints, even while hearing the sound of his mother's dead body rolling around in the trunk at every turn.

The reverend would be furious to find out that Naldo had left any loose ends. When he looked at the child, he felt he had no choice but to show him mercy. He couldn't explain it. He couldn't muster the courage to end his life. Naldo never wanted to disappoint Buddy. He could only pray the reverend never found out.

Naldo pulled the black Cadillac into an alleyway behind Saint Mary's Children's Home, and turned off the headlights. He removed the boy from the backseat and untied his bindings. Naldo perched him on the steps by the dumpsters and back door. He put his finger to his lips and whispered, "They will take care of you here, son." Naldo, made the sign of the cross and backed away from the child.

Naldo didn't seem to remember the boy blinking once. As he pulled out of the alley, the hair on the back of his neck stood up. The guilt from his disobedience began to set in. He desperately tried to put it out of his mind. He had a body to ditch.

* * *

FORT WORTH, TEXAS

"NICE WORK GENTLEMEN," CHIEF DRAEGER said. John Draeger had been the Chief of Police in Fort Worth for the last sixteen years. The roadmap of creases and lines below his vanishing hairline topographically depicted a career of tough decisions and unimaginable scenarios. He was pleased his two best detectives had, yet again, cracked the case.

"Thanks Chief," Tony said. "Let's hope he makes it to trial. Asshole didn't quite make it through that window too good. They'll be patching him up for a while."

"You boys get some rest," Draeger said. "There's plenty more where he came from. Donolla, I'm going to need a report on why you sprung to action before backup arrived. Write it out tomorrow so I can file something. Aaron, if you need a few days off, let me know. I know you got some personal things to deal with. Do what you gotta do."

"Im fine," Aaron said. "I appreciate it."

"Alright, see you nice and early tomorrow. Now, get out of my sight!" Draeger playfully motioned with a sweep of his hand. "Seriously, good work boys."

The two detectives walked down the hall to the elevator without saying a word. When the doors closed, Tony broke the silence. "Hey, you want grab a drink or something? I'm thinking about heading to Melnick's for a couple. Take the edge off. It's been a long few days. Come on, it'll do you some good."

"Thanks for asking," Aaron said. "I'm going to relieve the sitter and grab Scottie. I think we can make it to the hospital and get a little visit in. He needs to see his mom for a bit, I think. Next time, buddy. Have two for me. You have fun."

"Alright man, see you tomorrow. Give my best to Scottie."

When they arrived at the police parking lot, they went in opposite directions.

* * *

AARON HELD HIS SON'S HAND as they walked through the sliding glass doors of the hospital. He hated the way hospitals smelled, the bright lights; he hated everything about this place. He hated that this is what his life had become. Aaron did his best to hide his anger from Scott but he wasn't sure that was possible.

Scott walked beside his father with a spring in his step. His dirty blonde hair probably needed a comb run through it but his mom was better with those details than his dad. He'd had a fun day with the sitter, playing games and doing crafts, and now he was going to get to see Mommy. At five years old, he didn't quite grasp what was going on. He knew Mommy liked to sleep and she was just extra hard to wake up now. He was getting pretty eager for her to wake up soon. He had so much to tell her.

They checked in at the front desk, got in the elevator, and headed to the ICU. They walked down the long hallway to Heather's room. Aaron's anxiety and Scott's excitement heightened with each step. Aaron could hardly bear to see his wife hooked up to machines, unresponsive. The worst part was having to mask his devastation from his son. He had to be strong.

It had only been three weeks since Aaron brought Heather to the hospital. She had been complaining about headaches and dizziness and she could barely keep her food down from the nausea. Aaron figured she'd get some medication, change her diet, and come back for a follow up with a clean bill of health. When they arrived at the hospital, the doctors ran some tests then rushed her in for a CT scan. She was diagnosed with glioblastoma multiforme, the most aggressive type of malignant brain tumor. Four hours after her admittance, Heather experienced a massive seizure and slipped into a coma.

Aaron and his son arrived at Heather's hospital room. The door was closed so Aaron peered through the small rectangular window. He saw a nurse changing his wife's IV drip and his wife lying motionless in the bed. He inhaled deeply and closed his eyes for a moment before gently rapping on the door. The nurse looked up, smiled, and made her way over to them.

"Have you grown since the last time I saw you? I swear, you're getting bigger every day, Scottie," Nurse Rylee said, opening the door. "I think a big boy like you deserves a sucker. Would you like orange or purple?"

"Purple, please!" Scottie replied. "Purple is the color of monster boogers and 'eggprants' and I had socks that were purple on the bottom part and red on the top with a fish on it."

"I bet you did," Nurse Rylee said, cupping the back of Scott's head as he held firmly to her leg. She looked into Aaron's eyes, "I'll let Dr. Naidu know you're here." She put her hand on Aaron's forearm and squeezed before walking out of the room.

Aaron approached his wife's hospital bed. He looked down at her face; so peaceful, so angelic. He delicately drew circles on her hand with his finger, avoiding the taped IV needle implanted just below her wrist. He looked up to the ceiling, breathed in, and swallowed hard. His face contorted as he fought back the tears. He was hollow.

Scottie busied himself with the blinds on the far side of the room. Open, closed, open, almost closed, it was better than video games. He rolled his tiny red Mustang toy car on the inside window ledge, growling his interpretation of engine noises.

The doctor opened the door. He was a handsome man with jet black hair and kind eyes. Dr. Naidu finished medical school in Calcutta and went on to complete his six year residency in San Antonio. He spoke in soft, soothing tones with an accent more British than his native Hindi. "So nice to see you both. Hello Scottie, I like your car. I'm going to talk to your dad for a few minutes. You have fun playing, ok?"

"Good to see you doctor," Aaron said gruffly. He cleared his throat and continued. "Any good news? Anything changed? I'm kinda going out of my mind here. Anything would help."

"As we have discussed, Aaron, your wife is in very serious condition." Dr. Naidu lowered his voice, keeping his tone calm and comforting. He may have only had bad news to deliver, but his bedside manner was impeccable. "We are doing everything possible to keep the tumor from growing. She will need to have surgery very soon to remove it and if we are successful, there will be months of chemotherapy and radiation treatment. Hopefully, she will come out of the coma and, at the very least, you and Scott can say goodbye."

Aaron felt he'd been punched in the stomach. "How much time does she have, do you think?"

"Every patient reacts differently to surgery and therapy. Generally speaking it's about 15 to 18 months. Rare cases have gone as long as three years."

Aaron despised hearing his wife referred to as a "case", but he knew the doctor meant no harm. He fought back his raging emotions to continue a civilized conversation. All he wanted to do was scream and break everything in the room.

"Scottie, stop that!" Aaron lashed out. Scott had been driving his toy car along his mother's exposed arm up to her neck, and now he sat on the floor with his head in his hands and started to cry. Aaron ran over to his son and hugged him. He had never raised his voice to his son like that before. Aaron placed Scott in the cushioned chair in the far corner of the room and kissed the top of his head. "I'm sorry buddy, I love you. I just need you to sit here quietly for a little bit. Daddy needs to talk to the doctor. Hey, when we leave here, we'll go get some chicken nuggets and you can play with the other kids. That sound good?" Scott kept his head down and nodded slowly. Aaron walked back over to the doctor.

"So what you're saying, is the best I can hope for is a goodbye?" Aaron couldn't hide his red, watery eyes.

"That is usually the best scenario," Dr. Naidu explained. "This is a vicious form of cancer. It spreads quickly and it's impossible to remove completely. I wish I had better news for you, Aaron. I have to check on another patient. I'm so sorry."

"So that's it? Nothing can be done?" Aaron could no longer fight back the tears. He loved Heather so much. Aaron tried his best to keep his composure. Across the room, Scott looked up and ran over to his dad, hugging his waist tightly.

Dr. Naidu turned back to Aaron. "There are two doctors in Dallas that have made extraordinary strides in fighting this disease,"

Dr. Naidu whispered. "Everything is experimental, but the results have been very positive. It would be so expensive and no insurance would cover it. I don't want to give you false hope. If we can keep her alive long enough, well, you never know. I'm sorry, I shouldn't have said anything. I'm so sorry. I will see you on your next visit. Be strong for Scottie."

Aaron nodded, faked a smile, and picked up his son in his arms. With his free hand he tousled Scott's hair. "You ready for some chicken nuggets, buddy? Let's get some nuggets." Aaron kissed his son's forehead, looked back at his wife and started to walk out of the room.

"I love you mommy," Scott called over his daddy's shoulder.

Aaron bit his lip and closed his eyes, doing all he could to swallow the big lump in his throat. It was time for chicken nuggets.

* * *

THE BAR WAS DARK AND quiet, just the way Tony liked it. He'd knock a few back and head home to his wife. He was pretty sure she would love for him to wake her up from her drug induced sleep to talk about his day. Maybe it was time to make that baby. Maybe, he'd have another drink.

"Roy, another one if you're not too busy. A double this time and another bowl of these things. I skipped dinner."

Melnick's was almost deserted. A few patrons sat at the tables eating pretzels and telling lies. Not a bad crowd for a Thursday. A scantily clad woman in a denim skirt heaved her ample breasts onto the bar and ordered another spritzer. She looked at Tony and smiled.

Tony couldn't help but smile back. "Roy, I'll get that," Tony said. He raised his glass to the woman and took another swig.

It wasn't long before the woman moved a few seats closer. "Thanks for the drink, baby. I don't think I seen you in here before. Do you come here a lot?"

"Roy, do I come here a lot?" Tony asked.

"I can't get rid of him," Roy replied. "He's a permanent fixture."

"Hey, I ain't that bad. Yeah, I been here before," Tony said. "What's your name, sweetheart?"

"Whatever you want it to be, but Jennifer if you're getting technical. My friends call me Jenni, with an 'I'," Jennifer said.

"Sit a while, Jenni with an 'I'. Let's chat," Tony said. "Finish that, I'll get you another. Something better than spritzers, though. Get something good. Let's do a shot."

"Okay, that sounds fun," Jennifer said.

"Roy, two red headed sluts, por favor." It was the only fancy shot Tony knew. Roy reluctantly made the shots. He hated doing that shit. You want that, go to a nightclub. The new "couple" clinked glasses and downed their drinks simultaneously.

"You're cute," Jennifer whispered into Tony's ear. Her finger ran along the length of his thigh. She nuzzled into Tony's neck and playfully kissed his jowled jawline.

"You wanna get outta here, maybe?" Tony asked. "I was gonna have a few drinks but you seem like you might be done with that. Im just asking is all."

"You have a car, baby?" Jennifer asked.

"Yeah, out back." Tony said. "Let me pay Roy and we can get outta here." Tony placed two $20's on the bar.

Jennifer looked down at the cash and then back to Tony. "Make sure you save a little of that if you want to have a really good time." She gave Tony a smile as she moved her hand over the front of his khakis and squeezed.

"You're gonna be trouble, ain't ya, Jenni with an 'I'?" Tony chuckled, shaking his head. "A real wild one."

They stumbled together, arm in arm, into the parking lot. Tony was parked under a burned out street lamp at the back of the lot. There were only four other parked cars and they were nowhere near Tony's. The perfect spot for an impromptu rendezvous.

Tony opened the passenger door and Jennifer sat down. She swung her legs into the car. Her denim skirt hiked up during the maneuver showing Tony a short preview of the coming attraction. He closed the door after her, walked around to the driver's side, and got in.

They sat for a moment in silence before Tony moved a sausage fingered hand over to Jennifer's thigh. "One second, baby. Just a little financial matter before we get started," Jennifer said.

"Is this enough?" Tony said pulling out his badge.

"You're a cop? I knew things didn't feel right. A goddamned cop! Shit. I'm not doing this for free. Write me a ticket or take me to jail. Whatever. Won't be my first time. I'll be out by morning, you fat prick."

Tony reached into his pocket and pulled out three tightly wound small plastic baggies. "This might keep you there a little after breakfast, sweetheart."

"Your'e going to plant drugs on me, asshole?" Jennifer started to cry. "I can't believe this is happening. How can you do this to me?"

"How I see it," Tony began. "Things can go down one of two ways. I can take you to jail with these drugs on you," he paused.

"Or?" she asked, her voice trembling.

"I think you might be smart enough to figure out the rest." Tony unzipped the fly of his khakis and put his right hand around the back of Jennifer's neck. He wiped a tear from her cheek with his thumb. "I think everything's gonna work out, Jenni with an 'I'. Everything's gonna be okay."

Tony grabbed the back of her head and pushed it down toward his lap. He leaned back against the headrest, closed his eyes, and smiled. He could probably make it back in the bar before last call.

4

CUIDAD JUÁREZ, MEXICO

August, 1986

"SOPHIE, JUST GET ME THE usual," said the man in the white shirt, white pants, and matching fedora. "Don't forget the Valium, and see if you can grab me a few of those Flunitrapsiums, or whatever."

"Flunitrazepam," the small, redheaded woman said.

"That's the stuff. Thanks, sweetie. They help me sleep. Knock me out completely. Can you get me some of that Mexican vanilla too? That stuff is top notch. I'm just gonna hang out here and have a smoke. You got enough money don't ya?"

"Of course, Reverend. Back in a jiff." The woman opened the door to the farmácia and walked inside.

The man in white pulled out a pack of cigarettes from his shirt pocket. He pulled one from the pack and placed it between his lips. He reached into his pants pockets then patted his empty hands to his chest. A giant hand reached up from the street, holding a flame.

"Holy shit, son, you scared me half to death," mumbled the man in the fedora, his cigarette wagging in the air with every syllable. He didn't have too far to bend to meet the flame. With his cigarette lit, he stood up straight, took a long draw, and exhaled before speaking again. "What the hell are you sitting in the street for? I almost stepped on you, for Christ's sake."

The man on the ground was draped in a large grey and black pancho. He would have looked like a boulder covered with a blanket if his head wasn't poking through the top. An upturned baseball cap holding a few small coins lay in front of him. He peered up at the smoking man with sad eyes. "I see you are a man of God, señor. Can you spare any change? Anything would help."

"What? Change? Sorry, son, I don't do that. I don't like to encourage laziness, you understand? I do appreciate the light, so, thank you for that. What makes you think I'm a man of God?"

"You have a cross around your neck and that other lady called you reverend."

"Well, ain't you observant? Reverend Buddy Kind," he said, extending his hand without the cigarette toward the man on the ground. "And who might you be?"

The beggar looked up to see the bluest eyes he had ever seen. He froze for a moment, then fumbled underneath the pancho and brought his right hand out to shake the reverend's. "My name is

Naldo, Naldo Ortiz." Naldo clenched the reverend's hand and squeezed. He could see the man in white wince a little as they shook hands.

"That is one hell of a grip you got there, son," Buddy said. "You trying to tell me a guy with hands as strong as yours can't find work? Stand up for me. Let me get a good look at you."

Naldo shifted his legs and began to rise. He was now towering over Buddy and looking down at him. The door from the shop swung open and the small redheaded woman came running out frantically with a paper sack under one arm.

"You leave him alone!" she screamed. "He is a good man! You get out of here!"

"Calm down, Sophie," Buddy said. "Let me introduce you to my new friend here. This is," he paused, "What's your name again?"

"Naldo Ortiz, ma'am," he said, nodding his head slightly to the woman. "I mean no harm."

"I was just thinking, Sophie," Buddy said, "we could use a guy like Naldo here. Maybe he could be in charge of security and help put up the tent and stuff. Are you afraid of work, son? I don't have any use for a lazy sumbitch."

"You hardly know him, Reverend," Sophie whispered through gritted teeth while staring at him with wide eyes.

"What's to know?" Buddy said. "Look at the size of him. He's gotta be good for something. How tall are you, Naldo? 6'6", 6'7"?"

"Something like that, sir," Naldo replied.

"Hell, even if we need a stand-in just in case one of the tent poles breaks, he's bound to come in handy. Is there something wrong with you, Naldo? You stupid or something? We can work around stupid. Are you lazy? I just can't figure out why you're sitting in the dirt asking for money."

Naldo looked down at the floor and pulled his left arm from the pancho. He reluctantly showed Buddy his disfigured hand.

"Shit, that's all?" Buddy said, trying to hide his revulsion. "You get that thing stuck in a blender or what?"

"In some heavy machinery, sir, on my father's farm in Pánuco."

"Well, I'm not sure where that is, Naldo," Buddy said, "but you speak good English and you look strong as a horse. Are you interested in working for me, or not?"

Naldo dropped to one knee, fighting back the tears. He grabbed the reverend's hand and kissed it. "Thank you so much, sir," Naldo said between sobs. "I won't let you down. Gracias, señor." He looked up to the sky. "Gracias Dios."

"Alright, alright, that's enough fussin," Buddy said. "I take it you don't have any papers to get back into America. Don't worry about that, I know some folks. I got a little traveling revival show I like to do in a few small towns in Texas and New Mexico. It's not going to pay a whole hell of a lot, but I'll make sure you have food and a place to lay your head at night. We're getting set up in Marfa for a big revival this weekend. You ever been to Marfa, Naldo?"

"No, sir."

"Well, you ain't missed shit."

Naldo almost took up the entire back seat of Buddy's Cadillac. The dark tinted windows prevented the passing border guards with their drug sniffing dogs from seeing inside. They were at the back of a long line of cars waiting to cross into the United States. He knew this would never work. Two gringos driving a Mexican across the border was sure to raise some eyebrows no matter how nice the car was. Naldo was certain he would be back on the corner begging for change by tomorrow morning or perhaps a little later, depending on how long they detained him. The gap between them and the U.S. border was shrinking. He could see a guard ordering a car to pull over for a complete search less than ten cars ahead.

"Naldo, I think it'll be best if you just keep quiet back there," Buddy said. "Let me do the talking. People say I have a way with words. Ain't that right Sophie?"

"You certainly do, Reverend," Sophie said, smiling.

Naldo couldn't understand how they were so calm. There had to be repercussions for them as well. You can't just smuggle people across the border and hope for a slap on the wrist. He was regretting his decision to come along, though he didn't have much else waiting for him back in Juárez. After his accident left him unable to work on his father's farm, Naldo promised his family he would search for employment elsewhere and send them money whenever he could. So far, he had sent them nothing. He went from town to town, but nobody wanted to hire a cripple. A few months ago, after his 18th birthday, he was able to hitch a ride on a delivery truck from Chihuahua to Juárez. Naldo figured things would get better the closer to the United States he got. They didn't, and now he was as close as he'd ever been. Only one more car separated them from the guard.

Sophie turned back to Naldo and put her finger to her lips. He could hear Buddy's automatic window rolling down along with the sound of his heart thumping in his chest. Instinct made him want to open the door and run, but with one of his legs wedged behind the back of Buddy's seat, he thought better of it. Instead, he lowered his head and mouthed a silent prayer.

"Officer Gonzalo, it is sure good to see you again," Buddy said, greeting the guard. "How's the family?"

"They are doing fine, Reverend," the officer said. "Good to see you as well. Hi Sophie."

"Hi, Sugar," Sophie said with a smile and a dainty finger wave.

"Do you have anything to declare?"

"We got some more vanilla," Buddy said. "You know I love that stuff. I'm going to have to learn how to bake, I guess." Sophie pulled the large brown bottle from the paper sack and showed it to the guard.

"Alright, ya'll are good," Gonzalo said. He was about to wave them on, when he noticed Naldo in the back seat. He put his head inside the open window. "One second Reverend, just who do we have here?" Naldo's heart skipped a beat.

"This here's Naldo. I'm sure you've met him before. He's usually with us when we're passing through. He knows where to get the best street tacos in Juárez. Last time I came here without him, I had the shits for a week. Plus, he's got some distant relatives here. Figured we'd let him catch up for a bit while we were getting our vanilla. You understand."

"Do you have your passport, Naldo?" Officer Gonzalo said, peering in the window. Naldo began to tremble and he almost shook his head.

"Who carries around a passport?" Buddy interrupted with a chuckle. "I have his paperwork right here." Buddy reached out his hand to shake the officer's. From the back seat, Naldo could see a $100 bill palmed in the reverend's hand. "We'll be in Berino in a couple of weeks. I hope to see you there this time. Bring the wife and your daughter. Samantha, isn't it? I'll save you some good seats up front."

Officer Gonzalo put one hand in his pocket and with the other, waved the black Cadillac through the border and into the United States.

"Marfa is a couple of hours away, Naldo," Buddy said. "I hope you're comfy back there, cause I sure as hell ain't moving my seat up."

There was nothing noticeably different about the scenery on this side of the border, though Naldo couldn't stop smiling as it passed by his window. His bladder was bursting, and his left foot had fallen asleep miles ago, but he felt more alive than he had in years. He was seeing everything through new eyes. The sky seemed bluer, the cacti greener, and the landscape was the most delightful brown he had ever seen. This new world was brimming with hope, promise, and possibility.

They continued down Interstate 10 to Van Horn then went south on 90. The landscape was so flat you could see for miles in all directions. Hardly a word was spoken for most of the trip so far. They didn't make any stops along the way. There was probably a gas station in Van Horn, but Naldo didn't remember seeing one. The reverend kept flipping a cassette tape over whenever it came to the end of one side. Every time he flipped the tape he said, "Damn, I love me some Hank". Naldo recognized it to be country and western music but was unfamiliar with the artist. He was pretty sure Hank had something to do with it.

Naldo was trying to figure out why the man in the song kept crying in his beer, when the reverend turned the volume knob down and looked at Naldo through the rearview mirror. "You doin' alright back there, Naldo? We're almost in Marfa. Ain't it beautiful?"

"It is beautiful, sir," Naldo replied.

"Shit, I was just kidding, son," Buddy said. "If El Paso is the armpit of Texas, Marfa's it's asshole. When we get there, I'll introduce you to some of the folks you'll be working with and get you a sleeping bag and a pillow. We have some extra ones, right, Sophie?"

"I believe we do, Reverend," Sophie said. "He'll have to sleep under the stars, though, unless somebody lets him share their tent."

"Naldo, you have not lived until you seen the stars at night in Marfa," Buddy said. "Just watch for rattlesnakes. There's plenty of them too. We haven't had a casualty in the three years we been doin' this, ain't that right, Sophie? At least not due to snakes."

"You'll be fine, Naldo," Sophie interjected. "I think you're going to get on great here. It's like we're one big family."

"I cannot thank you both enough," Naldo said. A giant black and white tent swayed in the breeze only a few hundred yards in the distance. Buddy pulled the car off the tarmac and onto a dirt path.

"Naldo, I guess we're just about here," Buddy said. "Welcome to fuckin' Marfa, Texas"

Their entrance into the dusty parking lot was obstructed by a disheveled, long bearded man holding a large cardboard sign. The sign read, "REPENT! THE END IS NIGH!" in large red letters at the top. "Behold, I Am Coming Soon! My Reward Is With Me, And I Will Give To Everyone According To What He Has Done. Revelations 22:12" was written in smaller black letters underneath the red ones. The reverend tapped his horn, but the man refused to budge.

"Why do we always seem to attract these nut jobs, Sophie?" Buddy said, not expecting an answer. "Every place we go to we got to deal with one of these guys maybe once, twice a year, but Marfa never disappoints. I guess if it weren't for nut jobs we'd be outta business, huh, Sophie?"

As if to say, "Not in front of the help", Sophie gave Buddy a coy smile, but remained silent. Buddy honked his horn louder, drawing attention from the rest of the workers assembling chairs and tending to the grounds, but still getting no reaction from the man blocking their path.

"I guess I'll have a little talk with him," Buddy sighed and unfastened his seatbelt. "Just sit tight. I'll be back in a second." He got out of the car and slammed the door shut. Naldo rolled his window down less than an inch with the hope of eavesdropping on the exchange outside. He would have much preferred emptying his bladder, but Naldo had to admit, he was eager to see how it would all play out.

The reverend walked around to the front of the car. Naldo was impressed with Buddy's calm and collected demeanor. The man with the long grey beard said nothing as Buddy approached. Through the windshield, Naldo could see that the reverend was head and shoulders above the man standing next to him. With his hands in his pockets, Buddy looked down and kicked a pebble, then lifted his head to look down at the man before speaking.

"I think we might be in the same game here, amigo" Naldo could faintly hear Buddy say through his cracked open window. "I am also here to spread the word of God, and I think I might just reach a few more people than that paper sign of yours," Buddy continued. The man kept his stare forward to avoid eye contact with the reverend. Then Buddy whispered something in the man's ear. Naldo couldn't hear what he said, but he saw that the short grizzled man put his sign down to shake Buddy's hand. Their path was cleared. The workers up ahead near the tent resumed their duties.

Buddy got back in the car and put it in drive. "Sometimes you just gotta know how to talk to people," Buddy said. "Find out what appeals to their soul. He wasn't that hard a nut to crack."

"What did you say to him, Reverend?" Sophie asked.

"I slipped him five bucks and let him know that his 'end' was gonna be 'nigher' than expected if he didn't get the hell out of the parking lot."

Even Naldo was laughing heartily as they pulled into the parking space at the front entrance to the tent. Happy people were working diligently around the grounds. He saw the smiles on their faces. He could tell he was going to enjoy working for the revival and, especially, for the Reverend Buddy Kind. The reverend was a good man and Naldo was drawn to him; he owed his life to him.

Then, something slammed into the driver's side of the car. They all looked toward the sound and Sophie screamed. The man with the cardboard sign was back, hysterically yelling at the top of his lungs and beating on the Cadillac's windows with his open hands. His sign had fallen to the ground behind him.

"You're all going to Hell! God will smite you and your flock! You are aberrations in the eyes of the Lord! God will destroy you and your false prophet and you will be thrown alive into the lake of fire!"

"Time to put a stop to this once and for all," Buddy said, quickly pushing open his door. Although the screaming man was knocked over by the force of Buddy's door, he continued to scream his message as he writhed in the dirt. All the workers stopped working and stared at the spectacle.

"Ernesto, Steve, Dale, get over here and grab this guy, will you please?" Buddy said. The three men ran toward the car, two of them still holding their hammers. "There's gotta be some extra rope around here. I need you fellas to get this guy subdued, you understand? Put a bandana or something in his mouth. Someone's bound to have a bandana. I want to have a talk with him, but I don't think I necessarily want to hear what he has to say. There is no need to hurt our friend here, just get him tied up and leave him tied up outside my trailer. I'll deal with him in a bit." With little effort, the men restrained the protester and wrapped a sweaty bandana around his mouth. "Oh, and this here's Naldo," Buddy said motioning to the giant man now standing next to him. Naldo beamed while Buddy continued. "Look at the size of him. I think he's gonna get along here just fine." Buddy looked up at Naldo and said under his breath, "Follow me to my trailer. I'd like you to help me deal with a situation."

"I have a situation of my own, sir?" Naldo said, bobbing on his feet with his knees held tightly together.

"Jesus Christ, Naldo, you could have mentioned something earlier. Go take a leak at the back of the tent behind the dumpster and meet me at my trailer in five minutes."

"Thank you, sir." Naldo scampered away like a giant toddler with his shoelaces tied together.

After stopping and asking one of the workers for directions, Naldo was able to find Buddy's trailer on the opposite side of the property. The reverend leaned up against the side of the trailer, standing next to the man with the beard who was slumped over, almost motionless. The man was still bound by ropes but was much more subdued. The bandana loosely hung around his neck, allowing him to quietly babble something incoherent.

"Naldo, my boy, you found it. I'm proud of you. Now I got something a little more delicate for you to take care of."

"Yes, sir," Naldo responded. "How did you get him to calm down?"

"Well, he told me he was thirsty, so I got one of them pills Sophie got me from the pharmacy back in Juárez. I crushed one up and put it in a glass of water and, here we are. He'll be out like a light in a few minutes."

"Oh, I see, sir," Naldo said.

"Beware... false prophets... sheep... clothes... ravenous," slurred the man on the ground.

"Will he be alright?" Naldo asked.

"He's just taking a little nap, Naldo," Buddy said. "Shit, I think I hear him counting sheep. He'll be fine for now, but this is where you come in."

"I don't understand," Naldo said.

"I didn't figure you'd catch on right away. You see, Naldo, a guy like this is a cancer for us. We are trying to help people out here, give them hope, make people rejoice and bask in the glow of the love of Jesus. This guy starts screaming about the end of the world and how everybody's going to Hell and, well, it just doesn't fit in with the message we are trying to provide our parishioners. If anything, he stands in the way of us spreading the word. You wouldn't want that, would you Naldo?"

"No, sir."

"Shoot, I never even asked you, Naldo. Are you a Christian?"

"Yes, sir. I was raised Catholic." Naldo looked to the floor, ashamed. "I was close to giving up on faith until I met you today."

"That's great, Naldo. That's fine. So you can see how we need to rid our little revival of this sort of negativity, can't you?"

"Yes, sir."

"Good. Now we're on the same page, Naldo," Buddy said, slapping his knee. "I need you to take care of things. Get rid of this little situation for me. He's gonna be sound asleep in a bit. Get Sophie to get you the keys to one of the work trucks parked in the lot. Drive it over here and load this guy in the back. We are surrounded by desert here, Naldo. Get him as far away from here as you can without getting lost yourself. Take care of this and come back and tell me how it went. If you do good, I'll see about getting you your own tent."

"Yes, sir."

Naldo had been driving for about 20 minutes when he decided that he'd probably driven far enough. The scenery hadn't changed since he left Marfa, and every piece of desert looked as sufficient as the last for dropping someone off. Plus, he wasn't sure how long the reverend's pills would last. He pulled off the side of the highway and drove through the dirt. He wanted to be far enough away from the highway to make it unpleasant to walk to, but close enough that the man would be able to find his bearings and, either, walk or hitchhike back to his home.

He drove about 300 yards away from the road through the rough desert terrain, creating a wake of dust and debris. He thought this would be as good a place as any, so he stopped. He couldn't see the highway from where he parked the truck, but he was fairly certain the man would be able to navigate his way by just listening for the passing cars. Naldo couldn't remember seeing another vehicle in the last half hour.

Naldo got out of the truck and walked around to the bed. The man was curled up in the fetal position, still sound asleep. Naldo dropped the tailgate, adjusted some of the equipment and tools that were in the way, and dragged the man by his feet to the edge of the bed. He picked up the small man in his massive arms and gently placed him on the ground several yards away from the truck, careful not to set him on any sharp rocks or prickly plants. The man groaned and shifted when his head touched the dirt. Naldo removed the ropes and walked back to the truck.

Just before reaching the open door of the white Ford, Naldo stopped to say a prayer. He closed his eyes and grabbed for the rosary tucked inside the neckline of his shirt. He wanted to thank God for all his blessings today and pray for the safety of the man who lay asleep on the ground.

His prayer was interrupted when he heard, "Sinner!" screamed at him from behind. He turned quickly to see the man with the long grey beard only a few feet away, running at him with a short pocket knife held high above his head. Naldo instinctively put up his left hand to block his assailant. The knife plunged through the tough scar tissue lining his palm and stuck out the back of his already mangled hand. He reared back his right arm and punched the man, hard; his fist covering the entire landscape of his face. Naldo could feel the man's nose and teeth shattering from the force of his blow. His attacker dropped in an instant, then lay still, as blood spilled into the desert floor.

"Can you hear me?" Naldo called out as he stood over the inanimate body. He tried a gentle kick to the ribs, but the man didn't come to. His face looked like a squirrel feeding on raw hamburger. Naldo checked for a pulse and couldn't find one. The man was dead.

Naldo paced back and forth several times before realizing the knife was still embedded in his left hand. He winced for a second as he pulled it free in one quick motion. He wasn't thinking straight. He didn't know what he was supposed to do. Naldo dropped to his knees, put his hands to his face, and cried. His own blood poured down his face from the new wound in his hand. He stood up and walked over to the truck and found a rag and some electrical tape to stop the bleeding.

The sun would be setting in the next few hours and Naldo needed to figure out a plan of action. He couldn't just leave the body here. The vultures would be sure to draw attention from any state trooper that was passing by. He should have driven further into the desert. He could put the body in the truck and drive it further into the desert, but that would leave evidence. He was certain the reverend wouldn't want to be associated with any of this. Naldo would be sent to prison, or back to Mexico, or to a Mexican prison. He decided there was no other choice than to get rid of the body. How could a day with so much promise turn out like this?

Naldo fumbled in the back of the truck and found a post hole digger and a spade with a broken handle. He would make them work, somehow. The new injury to his left hand would have made the task impossible for most men, but Naldo wasn't most men. He finished the shallow grave within the hour.

With sweat dripping from his brow, Naldo placed the tools back in the truck and closed the tailgate. He looked back at the small mound of dirt he had just added to the topography. It looked unnatural, but he didn't figure anyone would come by here until it looked natural again. He got in the truck and paused for a moment to say a prayer, then stopped his prayer short. Perhaps, this wasn't the time to get the Lord's attention. Naldo thought he might be better off confessing next Sunday when he would be a little more presentable.

"Where is the reverend?" Naldo said to Sophie, obviously shaken.

"Sugar, he's in his office in the trailer on the left. You look like you seen a ghost. What happened to your hand? Is everything okay?"

"I can't talk right now. I need to see the reverend right away."

"He's back there, Naldo. Make sure you knock first. You might want to clean up a little too. You look like you've been run over."

"No time. Gracias, Sophie." Naldo knocked a few short knocks then turned the knob before hearing an answer. Buddy Kind was leaning back in his chair with his legs crossed on top of his desk, displaying his shiny ostrich skinned boots. His handgun was drawn. Naldo stood panting in the doorway.

"This better be good, Naldo," Buddy said, putting his sidearm back in his gun belt. "What took you so goddamned long? We have been worried sick. We have, I promise. Well, Sophie's been worried sick. She's a worrier."

"I'm sorry, sir. I came back as soon as I could," Naldo said between breaths. "I need to tell you something, sir. I don't think things went as planned. I did a very bad thing, but it was not my intention."

"Spill it, Naldo. The suspense is killin' me."

"Sir, I know you wanted me to take care of things so I drove him far away and took him into the desert. I untied him and I was going to leave him there."

"You untied him? Really?" Buddy questioned.

"Yes, untied him, sir," Naldo said. "And when I got back to the truck he was running at me with a knife. I tried to defend myself and he cut my hand. I punched him hard in the face and I think it killed him."

"You think?"

"No, I know, sir. I killed him. I'm so sorry." Naldo started to cry. "I was trying to do everything right. I didn't know what to do."

"What did you do with the body, Naldo?"

"I buried him out in the desert," Naldo said. "I can take you there so you can say a prayer."

"You done good. I don't think the prayer will be necessary," Buddy said, looking at Naldo's bandaged hand. "Let me take a look at that hand of yours."

Naldo pulled at the electrical tape and unwrapped the rag from his hand. He showed the fresh wound to Buddy.

"Man, right through the center," Buddy said. "That's not gonna help you with the ladies. Insult to injury, or vice versa. Does it hurt?"

"I haven't really thought about it, sir."

"You know, Naldo, it kinda looks like you got a touch of the stigmata," Buddy said. "I might be able to use that this Sunday. How do you feel about getting on stage?"

"Sir, I don't understand. A man died today because of me."

"It's all for the greater good," Buddy said. "Besides, what exactly did you think I meant by 'take care of things'?"

* * *

HE GASPED AS THE FABRIC filled his mouth, blocking his breath and jarring him to semiconsciousness. His left eye shot open. The right eyelid was slower to respond. His eyes rolled back and the lids closed again, one slightly after the other. He was forced to breathe in through his nose. The smell of must and old beer was overwhelming. His eyes reopened half way. Everything was black.

He had the sensation of lying down and standing up at the same time. His arms were extended far above his head and seemed to be locked in place by two metal cuffs. His ankles were similarly bound. He could feel the coolness of metal across both his knuckles, limiting the movement of his fingers.

Last he remembered, he was playing pool down at Nice Rack where the beers were cheap and the servers could be swayed to give you a little more than an eyeful, for the right price. He was on a hot streak, winning 40 bucks earlier in the evening then hustling a couple more patrons for another 60 before paying his tab. He remembered going out to his truck and deciding it would be best to take a little nap before heading back home to the wife, and maybe avoid getting nagged for coming home drunk, again. Everything after that was less than a blur.

He felt the quick tug of cloth being pulled from his face. His eyes adjusted slowly to his new surroundings as he tried to wipe the cobwebs from his addled mind. Someone in a black mask and hooded robe stood in front of him, staring, motionless.

With only cut outs for the eyes, the studded black leather mask revealed no emotion. The robed figure remained still. What the hell did I get myself into now?

Without provocation, the hooded figure began turning a large wooden crank just to the right of his abdomen. Only one revolution, at first. He could feel the metal of the shackles dig into the skin of his wrists and ankles. A few vertebrae popped into place.

Next, came a few twists of the screws atop the vises that covered his fingers like brass knuckles. His fingers stretched and separated.

Two more revolutions of the wooden crank. He'd never stretched this far before. He felt some pain in his shoulders, knees, and elbows. Red welts swelled around his wrists and ankles. His hips began to ache.

Three more twists of his knuckle vises and the throbbing pain was becoming unbearable. He stared back into the blank eyes of his punisher.

The crank was turned three more revolutions. An audible "pop" echoed through the chamber as his left femur ripped from the socket of his pelvis. He screamed uncontrollably. The man in the leather mask retreated to the shadows.

Sprawled out like a frog for dissection, he was helpless. He pulled against his restraints. Pain shot through him like lightning bolts. He screamed even louder in agony and terror. "Somebody help me! Help! Help me please, somebody!"

Out of the blackness, the masked man returned, a pear shaped metal object gripped firmly in his right hand.

Shit, Shit, Shit!

"Please don't do this!" he pleaded, tears streaming from his bloodshot eyes.

The metal pear was thrust into his mouth with such force it broke his two front teeth in half and knocked out the visible bottom row completely. He gagged on pieces of teeth and blood. He could no longer scream.

The maestro continued conducting his orchestra of torture. One more twist of the knuckle vise, and three fingers were broken and bleeding. Another turn of the crank, and both shoulders and right leg dislocated, loudly cracking like a three ball combination shot. The rotations and twists continued, slower now, building up to the final crescendo. One good turn deserves another.

His body was racked with pain. He slumped in his restraints, unable to move anything but his neck. He felt himself passing out. Blood spilled from his mouth and onto his chest. He was defeated.

The man in black moved in close, placed two fingers under his chin, and lifted. He was forced to look into his captor's eyes again. Like a dog listening to his master's voice on a recording, the man in the mask tilted his head, studying and assessing.

An ornate key protruding from the metal pear jutted out a few inches from his bloody lips. The key was turned clockwise in a complete circle, slowly.

He felt his jaws open slightly. The metal pear began to bloom. Four steel petals flowered in his mouth. Though his mouth was almost numb, he could feel steel pressing against the roof and on the gums of his bottom jaw where his teeth had recently been. His gaze was forced upward. He could no longer meet his captor's eyes.

Like winding up a children's toy, the key was now twisted rapidly. Each turn forced him to look upward to the ceiling. Four more cranks and a loud "crack" momentarily brought him back to reality as his jaw unhinged and swung loosely onto his chest like a trap door.

With the prick of a pin, the pain was gone; for now.

5

DALLAS, TEXAS

August, 1995

"WHAT'S THE MATTER BOY? CAT got your tongue?" The priest behind the desk at the front of the classroom asked, his Irish brogue hardly weakened by his 24 years in the States. Chuy sat quietly in his chair at the far corner of the room, next to the window overlooking the playground. He had spent many hours in the last two months staring out of that window. Unlike his classmates, he had no desire to be out there playing. He had no desire to be anywhere. He felt nothing.

"I've had enough of this nonsense, son," the priest said. "It's gone on long enough."

Chuy's eyes met the priest's. His face was expressionless. The priest was the first to break eye contact.

"See me after class boy. It's time a few things changed around here." The priest was notably flustered. "Students, get out your books and turn to page 115. Who would like to read it out loud to the class?" A young boy in the front row of tiny desks raised his hand without hesitation. "Alright, James then. James, 115 please."

Chuy shifted his gaze to the window. A handful of children ran around the playground as two nuns watched like buzzards to ensure that no one exceeded the prescribed dosage of enjoyment. James droned on in the background.

A bell rang and books slammed shut in unison. "Class, have chapters nine and ten read by tomorrow. I feel a pop quiz is long overdue," the priest warned. The children shuffled out of the room. Chuy rose from his desk. "Not so fast, boy. I know you understand me. We need to have a little chat." The priest was pointing at Chuy. "Come into my office, immediately." He stood next to the door behind his desk leading to his office, held it open, and with a quick jerk of his head, ushered Chuy inside.

* * *

"SIT." THE PRIEST GESTURED WITH an open palm to a black plastic chair placed in front of another desk. This one was larger and surrounded with bookshelves and filing cabinets. He looked down at the chair and then to Chuy. He raised his eyebrows and waited for Chuy to comply. The child sat down and the chair wobbled on warped legs. The priest walked around his desk to his cushioned leather chair. Chuy was dwarfed by the man behind the desk.

"So you show up here, uninvited, and you think you can make a mockery of me in front of my class?" the priest started. "We don't take insubordination lightly here at Saint Mary's. You got that, mister?" Chuy sat still and stared back which didn't seem to sit well with his teacher and he began to raise his voice.

"You're just there, all smug and quiet. I know you understand me you little bastard. I know you can talk." He rose from his leather chair, moved around his desk and stood in front of Chuy. "Stand up when I talk to you boy." He pulled on the back of his collar and Chuy was forced to his feet. The priest bent down and brought his face inches from Chuy's. The stench of stale cigarettes and communion wine wafted into the boy's nostrils and made his eyes water.

"We have ways of dealing with the likes of you, boy. It would be a pity if we had to blacken those beautiful blue eyes." The priest caressed the boy's cheek with the back of his hand. "Now stand with your face in that corner and don't move a muscle until I say you can!" the priest screamed. "We'll see if you can talk. You can count on that." He pushed Chuy's face into the corner and pushed once more for good measure then walked back to his desk.

The priest grabbed a metal ruler from a desk drawer and beat it against his open hand repeatedly as he sauntered over to Chuy. "Let's be honest, this is going to hurt you more than it will hurt me. All you have to do is tell me to stop. I want to hear you tell me."

The ruler whooshed through the air and landed squarely on Chuy's backside with a resounding "smack". The boy didn't budge. This was followed by several more swings of the ruler, each one harder than the last. The priest paused for a moment to catch his breath. Chuy stood in silence. The tears forming in his eyes were not from the pain.

Chuy felt the stubble from the man's chin brush against his ear. "You can't feel it because your clothes are in the way you little shit," he whispered. "We'll fix that. You can bet your sweet arse we'll fix that."

He tugged at Chuy's pants, exposing the six year old's bare bottom. Chuy's backside was red and swelling in several places where the edge of the ruler had dug into his skin. The man dropped the ruler, and slapped Chuy, full force, with his open hand. Chuy jerked forward, but made no sound.

The man extended his arm one last time and Chuy braced for impact. Instead, he gently cupped his hand on Chuy's right buttock. Bent over, with his nose close to the boy's left ear, he inhaled deeply and squeezed. "I have a sneaky suspicion you're going to feel this in the morning." He moved a hand to the front of the boy's pants and reached for the zipper.

Three quick knocks sounded and the office door swung open and another priest walked in. "What the Dickens is going on here? Get out of here, son! Go to your quarters."

"Just a little discipline Father. 'Spare the rod' you understand. I'll get through to that boy, someday. He has potential."

Chuy pulled up his pants and ran out of the office.

Chuy ran to the janitor's closet down the hall and slammed the door shut. He sat in the dark, arms wrapped around his knees. The scent of ammonia, disinfectant, and old mildewed mop heads swirled around him. With his head buried between his legs, he tried to be the smallest most insignificant thing in the world. He rocked back and forth, and cried. The dam had burst. He could no longer hold back the flood of tears and mucus spewing from his face.

The closet door opened. Chuy shielded his eyes from the light coming in from the hall. A man dressed in black with a white collar was looming in the doorway. Chuy trembled. He squeezed his eyes shut and pulled his knees in closer. A strong hand gripped his shoulder.

"It's alright now son. Nobody will hurt you." Chuy opened his eyes to see a kind face looking down at him. It was the priest that had interrupted his teacher's plans. He gently lifted Chuy to his feet. "There, there son. You'll be okay. Let's get you back to your sleeping quarters. You've had a bit of a jolt but it'll be alright now."

Chuy stared up at the man in silence. Chuy's cheeks were flushed and his nostrils were red and sore. One last tear trickled from his eye. It was the last one he would ever shed.

"Which dormitory are you in, son?" the priest asked. He waited for a response but none was given. "Is it A, B, or C?" Silence. "That's fine my boy. I believe you're new which probably means you're in A. We'll try that one first."

They walked down the hallway together, side by side. The priest cupped his hand on the back of Chuy's head, then let his arm drop to his side. Chuy reached up and wrapped his small hand around the priest's finger. They stopped in the hallway for a brief moment and stared at each other. The priest smiled openly and his eyes seemed to sparkle. Chuy looked up and his face relaxed as though a heavy burden was lifted from him. He felt six again.

They walked into the room with the plastic placard reading "Dormitory A" glued to the wall beside the door. 10 bunk beds lined the room, five on each side. Chuy led his new friend to his assigned bed and sat down on the mattress. The room was empty. The other children were probably outside playing or in one of the mandatory Bible classes taught throughout the day. The priest sat next to him.

"You don't speak much, do you son?" the priest asked. Chuy looked down and shook his head slowly from side to side. "Whenever you feel like it. No rush. I think you may have been through a lot. Life can give us many challenges. It's our job to work through them as best we can."

Chuy looked back up into the priest's eyes before laying his head against the man's arm. The priest patted him on the shoulder. Chuy closed his eyes, exhaled, and felt the corners of his mouth curve slightly upwards, involuntarily.

"We all need a little help sometimes, my son." The priest looked at Chuy as he removed the large metal crucifix from around his neck. He placed it over Chuy's head. "This is for your protection."

Chuy looked down at the cross and back up to the priest, shaking his head. The child swallowed hard and tried to clear his throat. "I… don't think… this… can help me," Chuy finally stuttered.

"Oh fiddlesticks!," the priest retorted. He grabbed the cross around Chuy's neck and held it in his hand. Chuy looked down quizzically as the priest put his thumb on the face of Jesus and pushed. A two inch blade shot out of the bottom of the cross.

The priest pushed the face of Jesus again and the blade retracted. He slapped Chuy's thigh twice as he stood up. "Everything is going to be alright, my boy. Everything will be alright." The priest winked and walked out of the room. Chuy clutched the crucifix and grinned.

* * *

FORT WORTH, TEXAS

"GLAD AT LEAST ONE OF you can make it on time," Chief Draeger said to Aaron. "If ya'll weren't so goddamned good together, I'd write him up. I'm going to get another cup, you want one Aaron?"

"I'm fine, Chief. Thanks" Aaron said. Draeger left the room and Aaron sat in silence. He could have used some extra sleep too. He hadn't slept well in weeks but he was a stickler for the rules. "If your not fifteen minutes early, you're ten minutes late," his father always said.

Tony burst into the office with half a bagel dangling from his mouth. He looked around the room, pleased to see only Aaron sitting there. He buttoned the top button of his wrinkled shirt and pulled a tie out of his pocket. He clipped it to his collar and sat in the chair next to Aaron then took another bite of breakfast.

"What's up buddy, did I miss anything?" Tony asked. Aaron dodged a few bagel projectiles and took a sip of his coffee.

"No, you're good. The chief'll be back in a bit. You look like you had a good night."

"Crazy shit, man. I'll tell you about it someday when you're old enough. No, I just got a late start. How was the hospital visit?"

"I took Scottie. It was difficult. Same old stuff. The doctor mentioned a," Aaron was interrupted by Chief Draeger's entrance.

"Nice of you to join us Donolla," Draeger said, sitting down behind his desk. "We have a couple of things to discuss here. First, hope you're both doing alright. I know it was a pretty big last few days. Good job, again. Now, I think we might have something a little bigger to chew on. We got some people going missing."

"What's going on?" Aaron asked. "For how long?"

"Its been at least a few months, maybe longer," Draeger said. "We never even thought it could be related. Shit, it may have been going on for years. We just noticed a correlation the last couple a days."

"Have there been any bodies found?" Aaron asked.

"Not yet, but we might be on to something. It reminds me of something that happened a while ago. I caught wind of it when I was a deputy back in Odessa. There was a string of people that went missing back in the 80's and 90's out in West Texas. This looks like there's is a slight chance it could be related. Like, maybe, the perp took some time off and just up and relocated. Who knows, really? Maybe there ain't just one. I guess I'm kinda grasping at straws here but the victims share some similarities. I'm hoping you boys can make sense of it."

"Give us the goods, Chief, " Tony said.

"There are at least 12 people that went missing last month either from the Metroplex or close by. Not kids or runaways. Pretty much middle-aged men from all backgrounds," Draeger said.

"People go missing all the time but it's usually women and children. So we decided to run some checks."

"What did you find out?" Aaron asked.

"Everything seemed unrelated at first. There were no similarities, so we ran all the missing people through our system. Every name had a ding."

"A 'ding'?" Tony asked.

"I think there's a common thread," Draeger said. "We didn't notice it at first."

"So what's the thread?" Aaron asked.

"Boys, I think we may be dealing with a vigilante. Every one of those missing people is a piece of shit," Draeger said. "We did a check on all of them and it didn't come back good. They're all convicted of something. Wife beaters, sex offenders, kiddie porn collectors. The lowest of the low. There isn't one that doesn't have a record of some sort. They're all terrible people from what we can see here in the computer, but they're missing, so we gotta see what's up. We don't know for sure if one missing person is connected to the next, but that's why I pay you guys."

"Are there any leads?" Aaron asked.

"Glad you mentioned it, Rider," Draeger said. "There's a guy who just got out of the ICU and put in the HDU out at Methodist. Every bone in his body has been dislocated. It may be nothing, but he also has thirteen counts of domestic violence. See if you can get anything out of him."

"We're on it, Chief," Tony chimed in. "We got this."

* * *

"LOOKS LIKE THIS ONE MIGHT be a biggie, huh buddy?" Tony said from the driver's seat. "That many people missing and no bodies? Sounds like maybe we got a professional we're dealing with. Do you know how to get to the hospital? What is it, Methodist?"

"I'm familiar with it," Aaron answered.

"Oh shit, is that where Heather is?"

"Yeah, she's still there," Aaron said.

"No good news then? Scottie doing okay?" Tony asked.

"As okay as can be expected, I guess. He thinks his mom's just in a really deep sleep. I don't know how to tell him she might not wake up. They're going to have to operate to remove the tumor, but even if that's a success, she probably just has a few months of pain and chemo. Doctor says at least we'll be able to say goodbye."

"That sucks, man. I'm so sorry," Tony said.

"The doctor says there's some experimental treatment that could help, but there's no way insurance would cover it and there's no way I'd be able to afford it anyway."

"We could have a fund raiser at work. I bet we could raise the money. Everyone would pitch in, I know it. We could spend this Saturday passing around a boot at traffic lights. We'll get the firefighters involved. I'm sure they wouldn't mind missing a foosball game or two," Tony said.

Aaron chuckled halfheartedly. "It wouldn't even come close, but I appreciate the support. What I need, is a miracle. If only I believed in miracles."

"That reminds me," Tony said. "Me and the wife are going to see that preacher guy I was telling you about, this Sunday. You should come along and bring Scottie. I've seen him heal people. Last week he told this autistic kid he didn't have autism no more. The kid started jumping around, all smiley and shit. Who am I to judge? I think it would do you some good. Maybe, say a prayer or two for Heather, and Scott."

"Thanks, I think I'll pass. Plus with this new case and all, I'll probably be too busy solving the crime. One of us has to do a little work." Aaron looked over at Tony and smiled. "Thanks, Tony."

"Suit yourself. I'm here if you need me. Hey, we could stop by Heather's room after we're done with this guy, if you like."

The smile faded from Aaron's face. "That's alright. I don't think I can do it today."

The yellow striped control arm lifted and they drove into the hospital parking lot.

* * *

THE TWO COPS LOOKED DOWN at the man on the hospital bed then back at each other, and shrugged their shoulders at the same time. The patient was wrapped from head to toe in plaster casts. Cables and pulleys held his limbs in place. He looked like a hospital scene extra in every sitcom ever made. Aaron and Tony couldn't help but share a smile. Aaron cleared his throat and regained his composure.

"Can you hear us, sir?" Aaron asked. "We are officers from the Fort Worth Police Department and we'd like to ask you a few questions."

No response. Tony took a pen out of his shirt pocket and poked the man's elbow. As if an ancient Egyptian tomb was being unearthed, the man stirred into consciousness with only grunts and groans.

"What are you doing to that patient?" a voice from the doorway asked. It was a doctor in a white coat holding a clipboard.

"We're from Fort Worth PD," Tony responded, showing his badge. "We're conducting an investigation and we need to ask this gentleman a few questions."

"I don't think this is appropriate right now," the doctor said. "Who let you in here?"

"The nurse at the front desk, with the hair and the glasses," Tony lied. "We just want to find out a few things and then we'll be out of here."

"Good luck with that," the doctor said. "This man has had every joint pulled from it's socket. His ligaments and tendons have been stretched and rendered useless. His fingers are so badly crushed he may never be able to write his name again or even push an elevator button. His jaw is broken in four places and is currently wired shut. And to top it off, he's on so many pain killers, he'd tell you he was the Queen of England if he could speak at all."

"So doctor," Aaron said. "Is there any chance this could be an accident? A car wreck maybe?"

"This man was left here in our parking lot, unconscious and bleeding. An anonymous call alerted us to his whereabouts. Somebody did this to him. There is no way this could be an accident. He has been physically stretched by some sort of device or machine. He'll never walk again, he'll always be confined to a wheelchair. He may never speak again. He must have made somebody very angry. This was no accident."

"Thank you for your cooperation," Aaron said. "We'll need to get a copy of the phone records for that night. Here's my card. Let us know if his status changes or if he's able to communicate at all. We'll find whoever did this to him. Have a good day."

The cops left the room and walked down the hall. Aaron closed his eyes for a moment and swallowed hard as they passed Heather's room on the way to the elevator.

* * *

FRISCO, TEXAS

FATHER DANIEL PLACED THE LAST bouquet of flowers on the burial plot. This was his favorite time. The flowers were donated by two local florists in town and, though the blooms were deemed unfit for sale, Father Daniel knew exactly how to trim and deadhead the arrangements so they looked beautiful. He felt it was important there were flowers on each gravesite every Sunday. Far too many people neglect their loved ones so soon after they are put in the ground. It's as if some don't even realize they're there.

Daniel stretched and took in a deep breath. He looked over his work and was pleased with what he had accomplished. He took out his pocket shears and snipped one last weed cowering behind the closest headstone. After mass today, he would fire up the riding mower and make everything perfect. The mower was given to the church by one of the parishioners. It needed some work at first, but now it ran like a deer. If it were up to Daniel, he'd be out mowing every Sunday morning at six. Father Quinn, however, didn't share Daniel's love for the blade or early mornings, so he resigned himself to mowing after mass.

With a few slaps of his hands, he brushed away the dirt and pollen. He pinched and pulled his pants at the thigh and stretched his neck to straighten his collar. Now, he was ready to pay a visit to Mrs. Fischer's Sunday school class. Father Daniel pushed open the creaky gate of the cemetery and walked toward the church. He'd be sure to oil that when he returned.

* * *

"LOOK WHO WE HAVE HERE, class," Mrs. Fischer said jubilantly. "It's Father Daniel. Can we say 'hi' to Father Daniel?"

"Hi Father Daniel," the students said together. It was music to Daniel's ears. He loved Sundays.

"And how is everyone this beautiful morning?"

"Good," the children chirped.

Daniel looked around the room at all the faces smiling widely, unrepressed by missing teeth. He noticed there was one empty seat in the back. There were also a few new children from the orphanage in Oak Cliff. It was common to have new children replace the ones that were possibly adopted or reprimanded for poor behavior. He welcomed them all to the class.

They sang "Jesus Loves Me" and "Jesus Loves the Little Children". Though lyrically antiquated, their messages were pure and the melodies were catchy. Father Daniel noticed that one of the children from Oak Cliff didn't join in. He didn't expect everyone to know all the words but usually the students would just mouth along and giggle when they got them wrong. The new boy looked frightened to be there.

The songs were followed by a quick question and answer session. Fortunately, no awkward questions were asked on this occasion. Father Daniel thanked the class for their time. He looked over to Mrs. Fischer who was sitting at her desk. "Can I see you in the hallway, Mrs. Fischer?"

Mrs. Fischer nodded her head quickly and leaped from her seat behind her desk. "Class, I need to talk to Father Daniel in the hall for just a minute. Ya'll continue in your Bible Study workbooks and I'll be back in just a minute. If you have an emergency, I'll be right outside that door. I don't want to hear any socializing while I'm out there." She followed Father Daniel into the hallway and closed the door behind her.

"Is everything ok, Father?" Mrs. Fischer asked.

"I'm not sure, Mrs. Fischer. I noticed one of the new children wasn't participating with the songs today. I realize that isn't a crime, but he seemed scared. Do you know anything about him? He was the one in the blue shirt."

"Oh, that's Adam, Father Daniel. It's his first day today. He came in from Oak Cliff on the bus with the other orphans. He might just be a little nervous. First day jitters, maybe. He seems like a nice enough kid. Not very talkative, though."

"If you don't mind, I'd like to speak with him," Father Daniel said. "Please send him out here. I want to meet him. Please make sure he knows he's not in trouble in any way."

"Ok, Father. I'll go run and get him. Just wait right here." Mrs. Fischer turned back towards the door and was about to turn the knob when Father Daniel stopped her.

"One more thing, Mrs. Fischer. I didn't see Luke in class today. Do you know where he is?"

"I meant to tell you," Mrs. Fischer started. "His step daddy got into to some terrible accident or something. I think he might've broken his arms and legs. We probably won't see Luke for a bit. His mamma said they might be moving to Oklahoma to stay with her parents for a while to figure things out. It was the darnedest thing. We just have to count our blessings while we can. Isn't that right, Father?"

"We certainly do, Mrs. Fischer."

"Is there anything else you wanted to talk about, Father Daniel?"

"That's everything. Thank you."

"Ok. Thank you, Father. I'll go fetch Adam for you."

As Mrs. Fischer entered her classroom, Daniel turned his back to the door and waited for Adam.

* * *

DANIEL TURNED BACK AROUND WHEN he heard the door open. He saw Mrs. Fischer escorting a reluctant little boy into the hall.

"Adam, Father Daniel would love to talk to you for a minute. Is that ok, Adam?" Mrs. Fischer asked. Adam's eyes met Daniel's and he quickly looked down at the floor.

"I wanted to personally welcome you to Saint Anthony's, Adam. We're so glad you could make it today," Daniel said. "You can get back to your class now, Mrs. Fischer. Thank you again."

As Mrs. Fischer retreated to her classroom, Adam raised his head and looked over to her. His big brown eyes followed her with a look that begged her not to leave. When she closed the door, the boy's gaze returned to the floor and he began to shake.

"You are safe here, my son," Father Daniel said placing his hand on Adam's shoulder. The boy flinched and Daniel took a step back. He realized immediately he wasn't dealing with "first day jitters".

"I'm here to help you if anything is wrong. Do you under-stand that?" Daniel asked. Adam shrugged but didn't reply. "I think you may be going through something at the orphanage. I can only help you if you tell me what that is."

Father Daniel used the wall to hold himself steady and bent his knees to sit cross legged on the floor. He made sure to keep his distance from the boy. He hoped Adam might consider him less of a threat if they could see each other eye to eye. "Do you want to tell me what's wrong, Adam?" After a long pause, Adam slowly shook his head from side to side.

"How about we do this?" Daniel continued. "I'll ask you a few questions and if you feel like answering you can either nod your head 'yes' or shake your head 'no'. You don't even have to say a word. Does that sound ok, Adam?" The boy hesitated for a moment, raised his head to look into Father Daniel's eyes, nodded, and stared back down at the ground.

"I want you to know you're not going to get in any trouble for anything you tell me today. Now, is there something going on back at Oak Cliff that you don't like?"

Adam nodded.

"Is there a person there that is making you uncomfortable?"

Adam nodded.

"Is this person a student?"

Adam shook his head.

"Is this person a teacher?"

Adam nodded.

"Does this teacher give you too much homework?"

Adam shook his head.

"Does this teacher yell at you?"

Adam paused for a second and then shook his head.

Father Daniel swallowed before asking his next question. He felt almost certain that he knew the answer. "Does this teacher touch you in any way where you don't want to be touched?"

Adam looked up and jumped into Father Daniel's arms. Tears were streaming out of his eyes. He cried uncontrollably as Daniel held him close. "It's alright my son, let it out," Father Daniel said in a soothing voice. "We won't let this happen again. If you can find the strength to tell us their name, I'll make sure it never happens to you or any other children again. Can you be brave for me, son?"

The sobbing continued for a few minutes until Adam finally cleared his nose with a big sniff and let out a long sigh. He looked at Daniel with bloodshot eyes. He studied Daniel's face for a moment before saying, "It's Father Doyle. He doesn't let me play at recess. He says that I'm bad and I have to stay and clean the chalkboard. Everyone else gets to play and I can't." Adam paused for a moment. "He makes me take my clothes off."

Father Daniel hugged him once more then stood up and extended his hand to Adam. The boy put his tiny hand in Daniel's. He led the boy down the hall to the administrative office and opened the door.

Sister Sarah was startled to see company this early in the day. She looked up from her paperwork. "Father Daniel, what can I do for you? Who's this?"

"Sister, this is Adam. I need you to make sure he doesn't get on the bus back to Oak Cliff today. Try to find a reputable children's home anywhere between here and Dallas. If there are no openings, put him on the list. If he has nowhere to stay for the night, I'll need you to make him up a room. I'll fill you in on the details later, I have some phone calls to make myself."

Adam wrapped his arms around Daniel's waist and squeezed. "You're safe now, son" Father Daniel said.

* * *

THE OLD KETTLE BEGAN TO whistle. Daniel turned off the knob on the stove and poured the hot water over a fresh teabag. He added three spoonfuls of sugar and filled the rest of the mug with milk. Daniel walked over to Father Quinn, handed him the tea, and sat down in the other armchair.

"Thank you my, son," Father Quinn Shepherd said. He took a long sip, gave a grunt of approval, and leaned back in his chair as if the antidote had just started to kick in. "Now what's this all about? What happened today that's gotten you all riled up?"

"I don't get it Father," Daniel said. "How can men of the cloth, men who have taken an oath of allegiance to God and to the church, hurt these children? How can the church let these men get away with it?"

"Give me a second to catch up, son. What occurred today?"

"There was a new boy in class today. He didn't seem to be acting right so I talked to him personally. He was touched inappropriately by a priest back at the orphanage. Who knows how long it's been going on for? How many others are there? Sister Sarah has made him a makeshift bed in the sacristy for the night, or longer. I'm not sending him back there."

"Rest assured, the offender will be punished," Father Quinn said. "Remember Ezekiel 18:20, 'The one who sins is the one who will die. The child will not share the guilt of the parent, nor will the parent share the guilt of the child. The righteousness of the righteous will be credited to them, and the wickedness of the wicked will be charged against them'. And Mathew 13:42, 'They will throw them into the blazing furnace, where there will be weeping and gnashing of teeth'. He'll get what's coming to him."

"How does that help that poor little boy?" Daniel asked, trying his best to keep his composure. He would never want Father Quinn to see him angry. "Adam is damaged now, and the church will just move Doyle Heffernan to another church or orphanage, or bible school. I don't see why this is allowed. Why do they just keep sweeping things under the rug?"

"I don't agree with all of it myself, Daniel. All of the coverups. It's an embarrassment to say the least. It pulls people away from the church and away from the teachings of Christ. Men were given freewill and men will always abuse it. The church tries to hide its flaws to preserve the message. It doesn't always work. Adam will probably have a tougher row to hoe than most. He has already been dealt an unfair hand losing his parents. In James 1:12 the Bible says, 'Blessed is the one who perseveres under trial because, having stood the test, that person will receive the crown of life that the Lord has promised to those who love him.' All of us are a work in progress. I truly hope this helps, son."

"Father, you have always helped me and have always been there when I've needed you," Daniel said. He breathed in deeply and exhaled as he tried to quell the surging waves of rage.

* * *

SOUTHLAKE, TEXAS

CAPACITY WAS 12,000 AND TONY couldn't see an empty seat in the house. He and his wife, Carol, arrived early to get good seats. They were only a few rows back from the stage, which was fantastic except there would be no sneaking out this week before the collection plate was passed around. A small price to pay, he supposed. They were close to the action. You never knew what Pastor Jacob was going to get up to. It was better than football.

"Good seats, huh Babe?" Tony said. Carol turned to him and nodded, feigning a smile. She wore a perpetual scowl as of late, like she was constantly smelling fish that was slightly off. She didn't much look like the woman he'd married, but he guessed a few years of putting up with his shenanigans could take its toll.

"We still got about ten minutes before showtime. You want a coffee or something?" Tony said.

"Yes," Carol said. "Caramel mocha frappe with whipped cream and a caramel drizzle. Oh, and some sort of danish. It doesn't matter what kind. Thanks."

"Jesus Christ," Tony said under his breath. "Coming right up my dear."

Megachurches these days were like mini malls. They had coffee vendors, food stalls, and tons of "church merch". The only thing missing was beer. Maybe he would write that suggestion down on the back the dollar bill he was going to put in the collection plate. He had to put something in to keep up appearances and there was no way he was parting with a Lincoln or Hamilton. He was pretty sure whatever the hell coffee his wife asked for would cost him a pretty penny anyway. They'd get him somehow.

He arrived at the coffee booth and got in line behind two women in flowered summer dresses. He couldn't help but admire their petite forms from the back. Smooth slender legs, asses like pearl onions, and just enough neck and back showing to take a mental picture for later viewing. The scents of lavender and cotton candy were hypnotizing. He heard one of them talk about how excited she was to finally get her driver's license next month. The other one mentioned how she'd be babysitting her little brother and working in one of her dad's sno-cone huts her sophomore year to save up to buy a VW bus.

"Jesus Christ," Tony said under his breath.

* * *

"HERE YOU GO SWEETHEART," TONY said, handing the coffee over to his wife. "They didn't have danishes so I got you a blueberry scone." Tony pushed the seat down and sat.

"Because a scone is just like a danish," Carol said. "Thanks hun. You want a scone?"

The lights flickered and everyone hurried to their seats. The room went dark and organ music started to play. At least 50 people in red robes started to assemble on either side of the stage. Cameras on cranes swooped in from the wings to get into position. Six camera operators captured the stage from every angle. Todays sermon would be seen by millions around the world.

"Ladies and gentlemen, Sowing Seeds Christian Fellowship is proud to present Pastor Jacob Dreyer. Put your hands together to welcome Pastor Jacob to the stage."

The choir began to sing. The orchestra played. It continued for about two minutes before fireworks shot out from the sides of the stage. The orchestra stopped and the choir hummed something beautiful. The curtains opened to nothingness. After a pause, the drums kicked in and the choir hummed louder. Something started to rise on stage. A giant wooden cross was being erected by hydraulics, front and center. There was a human being stuck to that cross, arms spread eagle, legs together. It continued to rise. When it reached its pinnacle, the humming and drumming stopped. The audience collectively gasped. The lights went out. A spotlight turned on, focussing on the cross. White feathery wings sprouted from the 'crucified' individual. Steel cables lifted him from his perch and gently placed him on his mark on the stage. The crowd went wild.

* * *

THEY WALKED THROUGH THE SEA of cars to get to theirs. It would be another hour before they would get out to the highway. The parking lot was like rush hour traffic. Tony mused how traffic reporters usually worded that the other way around. He couldn't help but smile thinking about it. He thought about sharing his little joke with Carol and then looked over to her in the passenger seat, and decided against it. Casting pearls before swine, plus she wanted pancakes.

"Man, that Pastor Jacob guy is good. I can't wait to see what he'll be up to next week," Tony said. "Worth every penny." When the collection plate was passed around, Tony was compelled to part with two George Washingtons.

They finally reached the exit and pulled onto the street. There was a little greasy spoon a few miles down the road they liked to go to after service. The food wasn't that great, but it wouldn't be packed like the fancier places closest to the church. Tony got a few breakfast tacos and his wife got the all-u-can-eat pancakes, ensuring the threat of conversation would be kept to a minimum.

6

DALLAS, TEXAS
September, 1995

CHUY WAS AWAKENED FROM HIS bunk by a knock on the door. The last thing he remembered was one of the nuns saying "lights out" before closing the door and leaving the room. The rest of the boys slept peacefully in their beds. Chuy rose to investigate.

He walked slowly between the rows of beds towards the door, gripping his blanket in one hand and dragging it on the floor. He passed bunk after bunk as the knocking continued. The room seemed much larger now. He felt he had passed at least 15 bunks and there were at least that many to go before he would reach his destination.

The knocking grew louder. Nobody stirred in their beds. Chuy was almost at the door.

"Who… is it?" Chuy asked sheepishly.

"I'm the pizza man. Open the door," said a guttural voice from the other side.

"I don't… think we're allowed to… have pizza," Chuy stammered.

"Open the goddamned door kid. It's a special delivery."

Chuy reached for the knob tentatively. His small hand shook. He twisted it slightly and the door flew open.

A giant figure in a black hooded robe stood in the doorway. His face was blackness. He had a cardboard pizza box raised in his right hand.

Chuy froze. The hooded creature discarded the box and approached the boy.

"I heard you ordered a fucking pizza." The monster was now only inches from Chuy's face.

Chuy finally found the will to move. He stepped backwards, stumbling over his feet and tripping over his blanket.

The creature pointed his left sleeve at Chuy. The bristled fore-limb of a praying mantis emerged from the arm hole, dripping with clear viscous jelly.

Chuy continued to step backwards. He tried his best to quicken his pace. The creature swiped maliciously at Chuy's face with an oddly hinged arm. None of the other boys woke up. The thing in the robe seemed to float toward him, faster.

He swatted away the attacks while rapidly running backwards as best he could. Then he slammed his back into something cold and squishy and stopped dead in his his tracks. Chuy could feel breath on the back of his neck. It was labored and cool.

He turned to meet his mother's gaze. Her face was purple and her eyes bulged out of her head. Her neck was broken and twisted. In a raspy voice, she gurgled, "You did this to me you filthy boy. You worthless, filthy boy! I wish you were never born!"

Chuy was immediately jarred to consciousness. His eyes were now wide open and he looked around his dark dorm room. He clutched the crucifix around his neck. He wasn't going to fall back asleep tonight.

* * *

"WELL CLASS, THE RESULTS FROM your exams are in and, I must say, you are all pathetic," Father Doyle said. "It's as if none of you listened to a thing I've taught you. How do you expect to become anything in life if you don't listen? Remember, no one wants to adopt a stupid child."

Father Doyle walked down the aisles of the classroom with a stack of papers in his hands. "Brian, '59'. A stellar performance my boy," the priest said sarcastically, slamming a paper on the boy's desk with the number "59" circled in red. "Jason, '64'. I would have expected a little more from the son of doctors. Just because they're dead, doesn't mean they can't be disappointed. Tyler, '46'. You would have done better spilling your ink on the page. James, wow, a '68'? I would have thought my star pupil would have at least passed. Maybe, spend more time with your nose in the books and less time with it up my backside."

The reprimands continued as Father Doyle meandered through the classroom. He had one paper left when he arrived at Chuy's desk. "Everyone, we have one exception," Father Doyle continued. "One shining star in the abyss. Chuy here has gotten a perfect score." He dropped the paper down on Chuy's desk. "100" was circled in red at the top.

Father Doyle leaned over the small desk and whispered in Chuy's ear. "I know you cheated you little blue eyed heathen. See me after class. Little boys who cheat on exams get punished."

The lecture continued until the bell rang. All the students got up from their desks and walked out of the classroom, except one. Chuy sat at his desk staring at his open book. The words blurred on the page as he started to tremble. There was punishment to be inflicted.

Chuy worked up the courage to knock on Father Doyle's office door. "Come in," said a muffled voice from the other side. Chuy pushed open the door and saw the priest sitting behind his desk.

"What took you so long? I thought I might have to hunt you down," Father Doyle said. "Sit." Chuy sat. "Now, I know there is no way you could have gotten a perfect score on that test, so I want you to tell me how you cheated so I can make sure it doesn't happen again. Your honesty here will save you a lot of grief, trust me. It's time to come clean."

"I…didn't cheat sir," Chuy said.

"You will address me as 'Father Doyle'. I'm growing tired of your impertinence. Don't challenge me boy. I will break you. Just admit that you cheated and I'll give you some extra assignments that you can complete in the next week. Lie to me, and I'll get my ruler. What'll it be, boy?"

"I didn't cheat."

"Right then, nose against the wall in the corner. You know the drill," Doyle commanded.

Chuy continued to stand in front of the priest. Father Doyle grabbed Chuy by his shoulders and shoved him into the corner. "Don't you ever defy me, boy! This is my house and you are just a guest. I can make sure you never get out of here. I have a lot of influence with the people who come here to adopt and with potential foster parents. 'Oh, I'm sorry that child is mentally retarded. He'll need constant care. You'll probably want a healthier one.' Just admit you cheated and we'll deal with it accordingly."

"I didn't cheat."

Father Doyle Heffernan went to his desk and grabbed his ruler. He walked back over to Chuy. "Take your pants down, boy," he demanded. Chuy stood still. "Take them down or I'll take them down for you." Chuy didn't move. "You don't want this, trust me," the priest warned.

Chuy felt his pants being forced down to his ankles. He could feel the chill from the air conditioner blowing on his exposed bottom. He breathed in deeply, awaiting the first strike. None came. He heard the unbuckling of a belt behind him. He squeezed his eyes shut as an arm reached under his belly and lifted him away from his corner.

Chuy was thrown on to the desk, his legs dangling inches from the floor. A strong forearm pressed against his back to limit his resistance. He could feel the tickles of leg hair pressed against the back of his smooth thighs.

"We could have done this the easy way," Father Doyle said. "But you decided to make it hard."

Chuy felt something warm and firm push against him from behind. He freed his right arm and reached for the crucifix around his neck. He struggled to push on the face of Jesus with his thumb and forefinger. The sharp blade shot out the bottom of the cross. Chuy was barely able to pull the rosary beads over his head while he back kicked his heel into Father Doyle's crotch with adrenaline fueled strength.

Father Doyle staggered back with his hands between his legs. Chuy flipped over on the desk and tried to pull up his trousers with one hand, while his other was gripped firmly around the tiny body of Jesus.

"I'm going to kill you, you little shit!" Father Doyle shouted, as he fought off the thrumming agony in his groin and tried to regain dominance. He limped towards Chuy with outstretched arms.

Chuy reared his arm back and plunged the crucifix into Father Doyle's right eye. Blood and clear intraocular fluid shot into the air and landed on Chuy's cheek. Chuy was able to administer another blow just below the punctured eye before the priest dropped to the floor and screamed. Father Doyle writhed in pain on his office floor, his own trousers were down and gathered around his ankles. Blood spewed from the wounds to his face.

The boy jumped off the desk and pulled up his pants. Chuy saw the priest flop around on the floor like a fish out of water. He backed away from Doyle and watched. When the moment was perfect, Chuy took a running start and swiftly planted his size 1 dress shoe between the priest's legs as hard as he could. Father Doyle buckled with the force of the impact. His face was a bloody mess and he was no longer able to see his attacker. Chuy pounced on the priest's chest, knees first. He put his face dangerously close to Doyle's sputtering mouth; his tiny dagger drawn and held tightly against the man's neck. Chuy jerked Doyle's head to the side so he could speak directly into his ear.

"You are a bad man. Don't ever try to do this to me again. Don't do it to any of the other children either, or next time I'll kill you. Do you hear me?" Chuy asked.

Despite the pain that wracked his face and body, Father Doyle found the strength to nod his head in compliance. Chuy pushed his head to the floor and stood up.

"What's the matter Father, cat got your tongue?"

Chuy opened the door and walked out of the office.

* * *

THE SOUND OF SIRENS FADED as the ambulance turned the corner and headed to the hospital. Chuy watched the bright lights disappear down the street from the window of his dorm room. He sat on top of his neatly made bunk and stared out the window. He was alone in the dorm for now but he heard footsteps coming down the hallway then a door creaking open. Chuy didn't bother to look up to see who it was. At this point, he didn't really care.

"You've had yourself quite a day, haven't you son?" said a kind voice. Chuy looked away from the window to see the priest that had given him the crucifix standing next to him. The man sat down on the bed next to Chuy. "Everything is all right now."

"He deserved it. He's not a good man," Chuy said.

"He deserved every bit of it my boy. And then some." The priest patted Chuy's knee.

"How much trouble am I in?" Chuy asked.

"Trouble? For what, son? Your have done nothing wrong, and Father Doyle was quick to tell the paramedics how he had tripped in his office and fallen on his scissors. So clumsy of him. You'd think he'd be more careful."

The two shared a secret smile. The priest put his hand on Chuy's shoulder. "As long as I am able, I will make sure that no one ever hurts you again. You are safe now, my son."

Father Quinn was always true to his word.

* * *

FORT WORTH, TEXAS

"IT'S PROBABLY A LONG SHOT," Chief Draeger said, "but we've dug up a few things, opened a few cold cases and if they don't have anything to do with these new missing people, they got something to do with something."

"Chief, you're talking in riddles here," Tony said. "Can you spell it out?"

"Yeah, I'll try to dumb it down a bit for you, Donolla," Draeger continued. "I told you about the hunch I had before, but I'll refresh your memory. 21 people went missing in the late 80's and 90's from the Texas cities of Marfa, Alpine, Terlingua, El Paso, and also Berino and Las Cruces, New Mexico. Nobody made a connection and, hell, I'm still not 100% sure there is one. But in 1995, this single mom from El Paso came to Dallas and she's never heard from again. Her kid gets dropped off at a local orphanage. They called the cops from the orphanage and they try to to talk to the kid, but he ain't saying shit. Like he's mute or something. Luckily, he was wearing an I.D. bracelet. The lady had no family. The cops got a clue when they got a call from this motel manager saying a lady left all her stuff in the room and she never dropped off the key at check out. She had signed in under the name Lupe Verdugo and she had a small boy with her. There was no evidence worth a dam at the motel room so they pretty much chalked it up to child abandonment. Single moms lose their minds sometimes. Anyway, there was a halfhearted search and she was never found."

"And this makes you think it's connected to our new missing person cases, how?" Tony interrupted.

"Let me finish, Donolla. The phone records were overlooked or, at least, not looked at carefully. The last call from the room was to a pizza place. The cops got in touch with the restaurant and they said they sent a delivery guy to the motel that night but nobody answered so he brought the pizza back to the shop. We were going through some cold case files on missing persons and we came to hers. There were three other calls made that day from that motel room. All three of them went to Reverend Kind's Christian Experience. It was some sort of faith healing evangelist bullshit church in a mini mall."

"Now I think I'm lost, Chief," Aaron said.

"Wait for it Rider. Jesus, just listen. I feel like I'm doing all the work for you here, boys," Draeger said. "The church was led by the Reverend Buddy Kind. Before he came to Dallas he was a traveling preacher in one of them tent shows that moves from town to town getting people's money for prayers. He used to travel to Marfa, Alpine, Terlingua, El Paso, Berino, and Las Cruces."

"I think I'm seeing a pattern, Chief," Tony said.

"Glad to see the light bulb hasn't completely burned out," Draeger said. "Now these folks that went missing were all adults but some of them were women which I know doesn't quite fit our new perp's M.O., if we even have a perp. But it does seem that wherever the Reverend Buddy Kind shows up, people go missing."

"So how do we get in touch with this Buddy Kind?" Aaron asked. "Is he still here in Dallas?"

"That's the tricky part," Draeger said. "He's still here alright, but he no longer goes by Buddy Kind. He uses his real name now. He's running the megachurch out in Southlake."

"Wait," Tony said "Jacob Dreyer is our suspect? Me and the wife just went to see him Sunday. You serious? Jacob freaking Dreyer?"

"I know it's hard to take it all in," Drager said. "This is a dicey situation. If he catches wind that we're snooping around he'll shut us down in a second. That boy's got more money than God. He'll set his lawyers on us and sue us for defamation of character or anything he wants to. It would be a goddamned media circus. We have to gather some evidence. We have to be certain. He may not be guilty of this, but you can be damned sure he's guilty of something."

"We're on it, Chief," Aaron said.

"One more thing," Dreager said. "We tracked down the boy who was dropped off at the orphanage. He's the priest at a small church in Frisco. Saint Anthony's Catholic Church. See if he remembers anything about his mom or what happened back on the day his mom disappeared. Hopefully, he can talk now. His name is Father Daniel Jesus Verdugo. He used to go by Chuy. I think it's Spanish for Jesus or something. Anyway, do some investigating and keep me posted. You can call it a day for now, but I want something we can work with in the next few days."

"Have a good one, Chief," Tony said.

"We won't let you down, Chief," Aaron added.

* * *

TONY WALKED OUT TO HIS car in the parking lot and got in. He started up the car and sat there for a moment to let the air conditioning kick in to the optimal temperature for driving. He pulled out his phone and looked up Sowing Seeds Christian Fellowship, and dialed the number.

"Thank you for calling the Sowing Seeds Christian Fellowship prayer line, this is Trish, how can I assist you with your prayer today?" an overly enthusiastic voice said.

"I'm trying to get a hold of Pastor Jacob Dreyer, please," Tony said.

"Sir, this is a prayer line. If you have anything you would like Pastor Jacob to pray about for you, I will write it down and make sure that the Pastor prays for you," Trish said. "We also have a recurring Sowing Seeds of Faith plan that is only $77 a month. Would you be interested in that or would you prefer a one time donation, sir?"

"No thanks, I need to get a hold of the pastor. Can you give me a number so I can reach him? It's important."

"I'm sorry, I can't give out that information, sir. If I can get your name and address, I can send you some information about how our congregation works and how we can help you get closer to God. What's your name, sir?"

"Hey Trish, I'm good. Thanks for nothing." Tony hung up. "Eager bitch."

Tony scrolled through internet on his phone a little longer and found a few more numbers for the offices of Jacob Dreyer. He went down the list. Most of them went to voicemail; the others were answered but he was redirected to different answering services. He'd almost given up when the last number he called was answered by a friendly voice.

"Office of Pastor Jacob Dreyer, this is Sophie, how can I direct your call?"

"Sophie, finally, how are you sweetheart? Im trying desperately to get a hold of Jacob Dreyer."

"The pastor is busy at the moment, can I take a message?"

"Look Sophie, this is Detective Anthony Donolla of the Fort Worth Police Department. I have some information I think the pastor is going to want know about. Tell him to call me when he can.

It'll be super important for him to follow up on this one." Tony left his cell phone number before hanging up.

Less than two minutes later, Tony's phone rang. It was the pastor. He let it go to voicemail, just to be a dick.

7

DALLAS, TEXAS

April, 2001

"BEFORE WE GET STARTED WITH practice today, who can tell me the first of our five guiding principles for karate?" asked the man in the white karate gi wrapped with a black belt. The class looked back it him with blank faces. "No one here can tell me the first principle? I know you guys know this. We go over this every week."

Chuy was kneeling on the mat, sitting on his feet along with the other children in the class. He was nearly the smallest boy in the room; second only to a frail, red headed, freckled child who was kneeling near the back of the class. The boy, David, was three years older than Chuy and generally kept to himself. Chuy didn't get the impression that David wanted to participate in karate class, whatsoever. Before class, Chuy saw him trying to get back inside his mother's mini van as she locked the doors and sped off. David always showed up to class with watery eyes that matched his hair.

Even though Chuy was only 12 years old, Sensei Glenn thought it would be best for him to train with the 13 to 16 year olds. "I'd only be holding you back, Chuy," his sensei had told him, "You're too advanced for the kiddie classes." Chuy didn't feel advanced. He was a bit of a late bloomer and now he was the youngest boy in a dojo full of 'men'. The kid next to him had a five o'clock shadow. Chuy reluctantly raised his hand.

"Finally," Glenn said, frustrated. "Chuy, do you know the first principle for karate?"

"Um, yes, Sensei."

"Alright, what is it, Chuy?"

"'Character'," he answered.

"That's right, Chuy. Class, we are always seeking perfection of 'Character'. It doesn't matter if we win or lose, it's just important that we try. The only way you can fail is by quitting. Does everyone understand?"

"Yes, Sensei," the group shouted back with enthusiasm.

"Okay, anyone want to try for the second principle?" Glenn looked around the room and saw only one boy with his hand half raised. "Chuy, then, what's the second principle?.

"'Sincerity'," Chuy said.

"Very good, Chuy. 'Sincerity' is being faithful to ourselves in everything we do. If we can deal with others with 'Sincerity' , we start to build a feeling of trust and mutual respect with them. Be honest and sincere and try to be the best person you can be. Now, who knows the third principle? Anyone?" Glenn asked.

Chuy didn't raise his hand immediately. The sensei scanned the room to find other willing participants first. He saw none, then looked back to Chuy.

"'Effort,'" Chuy said, not wanting to let his sensei down.

"Yes, 'Effort,'" Glenn said with a sigh. "This seems to be the one everyone, except Chuy, is forgetting. It's not that hard, people. Your parents are taking valuable time out of their day to get you here. The least you could do is put in a little 'Effort'. Chuy, just tell everyone the last two principles so we can get on with class."

"'Self-Control' and 'Courtesy', Sensei,"

"Excellent, Chuy. Thanks for being the only one who seems to be able to pay attention."

"Why don't you get your nose out of Sensei's asshole?" Chuy heard a boy whisper behind him. He wasn't exactly sure what that was supposed to mean. He'd heard something like it once before and he could tell the boy wasn't being friendly. Chuy knew the one behind him to be Carlos. He was probably the tallest kid in the class, or at least the heaviest. Carlos was big and ugly. His dark, bushy eyebrows connected in the middle and the acne on his face looked like strawberry preserves spread on whole grain toast. Chuy ignored Carlos' comment and kept his focus on Sensei Glenn.

"So 'Self-Control' is a reminder to stay calm," Glenn continued. "We have to be in control of our mind, our emotions, and our actions, at all times. Avoid violent behavior in every situation when you can. Karate is self defense, not just a way to beat up your enemies. Lastly, 'Courtesy'. We need to be courteous to one another. Remember the 'Golden Rule'. 'Do unto others as you would have others do unto you'. Now please be courteous to me and your fellow classmates and have the principles memorized for next week for goodness sake. Do you understand class?"

"Yes, Sensei!" the class answered.

"Good, now let's get down to some karate. Everyone, pick a partner and find some room in the dojo to practice sparring. If you can't find a partner, I will find one for you."

"Yes, Sensei!"

The boy next to Chuy asked if he'd like to be his partner. Aside from the beard stubble, Chuy felt they were suitably matched in height, weight, and belt color. The two found an empty area in one corner of the dojo and stood facing each other, waiting for Sensei Glenn's instruction. Carlos had been paired up with David, the scrawny red head. David's legs were visibly trembling and Carlos looked like a ravenous bulldog preparing to feast on his first course. Certain these two didn't pick each other to spar against, Chuy realized this was one of the many hazards of being different.

Father Quinn signed Chuy up for karate almost a year ago. He thought it would be good for him to experience something other than the rusty monkey bars and searing, metal slide offered at the orphanage. Father Quinn believed some self defense would come in handy. He said that boys Chuy's age shouldn't be all cooped up together in a dormitory; that 12 year old boys were raging with hormones and couldn't be trusted. Chuy knew rage, but he didn't think it had to do with hormones. They weren't teaching him anything about puberty at Saint Mary's, but he could tell that some of his bunk mates squeaked when they talked and got really mad if he walked into the bathroom stall without knocking. Chuy thought he saw a hair under his arm a week ago, but it turned out to be a stray thread from his shirt.

Chuy had become very attached to Father Quinn over the last six years. The priest was the only person who made him feel safe. Father Quinn promised when the time was right, he would have Chuy move in with him at Saint Anthony of Padua Catholic Church in Frisco. He'd been able to take a few day trips there to help out with bake sales and clothing and toy drives, but the orphanage was very strict on overnight stays. He guessed they would rather he swam with the sharks. Chuy wanted to be just like Father Quinn when he grew up, and he thought Frisco must be the most beautiful place in the world. When he was dropped off at karate today, Father Quinn told him he'd take him for ice-cream after class. Chuy was excited, but it didn't mask the dread of having to return to the shark infested waters of the orphanage.

"Everyone paired up?," Sensei Glenn asked, looking around the room. "Very good. Now bow to your opponent. Remember, no physical contact. Don't hit the person, just throw a punch or kick at him and let him block it. Go very slowly at first. Once you get your rhythm, you can move faster. Understand?"

"Yes, Sensei!"

"Good, and when you punch or kick remember to shout 'kiai'," Glenn instructed. "It means focus your life force. That's what I want you to do. Focus, people. Remember your breathing. Good form, Robert, keep it up, guys. I need to make a phone call. I'll be back in a second. Keep up the good work."

They practiced their drills for only several minutes before a commotion in the middle of the room stopped everyone from sparring. David was doubled over on the floor crying and Carlos stood over him, spitting on him. "You leave him alone!" Chuy screamed as he ran from the corner. He pushed Carlos hard, knocking him to the padded mat. Chuy grabbed David under the arms to help him to his feet. Sensei Glenn saw the tail end of the altercation from his glass enclosed office, and bolted over to investigate. Carlos managed to stand back up on his feet. He approached Chuy and pushed his hands into his chest.

"What in God's name is going on here?" Glenn asked, separating the boys by standing between them.

"That little faggot tried to grab my dick so I leveled him," Carlos said, pointing at David. "I will kick that dude's ass if he tries that again."

"Watch your language, Carlos," Glenn said. "Are you alright, David?"

David couldn't make eye contact with Sensei Glenn or anyone else in the room. He was hyperventilating and convulsing between his bouts of snotty blubbering. "My hand slipped and he punched me in the stomach," David finally managed to say.

"This guy here better watch himself too," Carlos said, pushing Chuy again, harder this time.

Chuy stumbled back on his heels for a moment before regaining his balance and charging back at Carlos. Carlos was ready for impact and his massive body hardly budged.

"Calm down boys," Glenn intervened, standing between them again. "David, go to my office. I think you're going to live. I'll call your mother to come pick you up in a few minutes." He turned his attention to attention to Chuy and Carlos. "What the heck has gotten into you two? I want you to settle this with what you've learned in karate. Remember the five principles. Class, make a circle in the middle of the dojo. Chuy, Carlos, take a few breaths. When you're both ready, step into the circle. This isn't about beating each other up, it's about seeing who has more control. No contact. I will be referee and judge. Best of three rounds. Let's go fellas."

Chuy stepped into the circle, surrounded by his classmates. He looked at his opponent, suddenly noticing the yellow belt around his waist was one level lower than Carlos' orange. He tried to remember all the blocks, kicks, and punches, he learned over the last year. Chuy couldn't remember a single lesson. The rest of the class gossiped under their breaths. Carlos stood up straight and puffed out his chest, trying to look as mean as possible.

"Bow to each other." They complied with their sensei's request. "Ready. Begin," Sensei Glenn said, swinging his arm down in a chopping motion.

Carlos stood still. Chuy cautiously made his way over to the other side of the ring. He threw a punch that was easily blocked and Carlos brought his knee up into Chuy's abdomen. His knee never made contact, but it was obviously a victory to Carlos for that round.

"One point, Carlos," Sensei Glenn said. "Bow. Round two."

In the second round, Carlos was more aggressive. He galloped over to Chuy with one leg behind the other. Chuy studied his face. When Carlos punched, Chuy ducked and crouched while sweeping at Carlos' left calf before stopping just short of impact.

"Point. Chuy," Glenn said. "This next round decides the match. Nice job, gentlemen. Before this last round, I want you to bow and shake hands. Remember it's not about who wins. It's about 'Character', 'Sincerity', 'Effort', 'Self-Control', and 'Courtesy.'" Both of the young fighters made their way to the center of the dojo. Chuy looked up into the face of his opponent and extended his hand for the handshake.

Carlos declined Chuy's hand and, instead, leaned in and whispered in Chuy's ear, "I heard your whore mother hated you so much, she dropped you off at the orphanage and killed herself 'cause she couldn't stand to look at you." Carlos smiled, pleased with what he had said.

"Ready. Begin."

Chuy locked eyes and slowly made his way over to Carlos. Carlos started to swing, but Chuy ducked and pivoted his leg before delivering a magnificent roundhouse kick. Chuy's toes swept across Carlos' face, wiping away his smirk, and cracking his nose in several places. Blood started to pour out of Carlos' face as he fell to the mat. Chuy was on top of him in an instant. With his left hand, he grabbed a clump of black hair on the top of Carlos' head, he pulled his face up to meet his downward fist, then slammed the back of his head to the floor. He repeated the process as many times as he could before Sensei Glenn jumped on top of him and wrenched him off. David was craning his neck and smiling from his limited vantage point in the dojo office. Carlos remained on the mat. He was crying like an infant and holding his hands up to cover his bloody face.

"So karate class was good today?" Father Quinn asked when Chuy got into the van. He knew it hadn't gone well from the phone call he received from Sensei Glenn only 20 minutes prior. He got there as quick as he could.

"It was okay," Chuy said. "There was a bit of a thing, but I think it'll be alright."

"A thing, eh?" Quinn asked. "What kind of thing?"

"I mean, there was a kid there that tried to fight me for real, but then I fought him and it was just a thing, I guess."

"I know what happened, son. I talked to Sensei Glenn. He said the other guy was a brute and he actually deserved it. I'm not mad at you. You know that, right?"

"I guess I do," Chuy said.

"There are a few times in this life when we have to use violence to make things right. You can do unto others as much as you'd like to have done to you, but if those same people are doing horrible things to other people, you have to stop it."

"I feel like I lost control, Father," Chuy said.

"You took control, son, and you won. You did what was right and fair. I've never been more proud of you, my boy."

Chuy noticed they were taking an unfamiliar route back to the orphanage and asked "Where are we going, Father? I don't remember going this way before."

"I promised you ice-cream, didn't I?"

"You did, but I don't think I deserve it."

"Nonsense. Everyone deserves ice-cream sometime, and after ice-cream, we're headed to Frisco. Would that be okay with you, Chuy?"

"It's more than okay, Father. Will they let me back into Saint Mary's tonight? I don't want to get in more trouble than I'm probably already in."

"You're going to stay at the church for the weekend," Father Quinn said. "It's a trial basis, but they said you could. Are you okay with that?"

Chuy turned and looked at Father Quinn in shocked disbelief. "Seriously?"

"Seriously."

Chuy closed his eyes. His smile became awkward and distorted. He felt like crying but was able to control his emotions. No one could ever see even a hint of vulnerability.

* * *

SOUTHLAKE, TEXAS

"THIS IS PASTOR JACOB DREYER returning your call. Please call me back at your earliest convenience. This is my private number so it should reach me directly. Thanks." He hated leaving voicemails.

Jacob sat behind a huge mahogany desk. He rearranged some papers and straightened the pens in the pen holder. He didn't really have anything to do at his office. Jacob showed up there a few times a week just to feign some interest in the inner workings of his ministry. This was all the "behind the curtain" stuff. He was the face of the operation; the front man; the showman. He was the reason those seats were filled every week. All the cogs and gears were of no importance to him. His cell phone rang.

"Jacob Dreyer," he answered.

"Yeah, Pastor Jacob, this is Detective Anthony Donolla, Fort Worth P.D."

"How are you, sir? What can I do you for?" Jacob said.

"I'm doing good. Look, I got some information about some things that might concern you. I'd rather not talk about it over the phone. Is there a time and place that would be convenient for us to have a little chat?"

"I'm a very busy man, Detective," Jacob said. "You can just send over whatever paperwork or whatever you need to tell me, to my secretary, Sophie. She handles all my business. She'll make sure it gets taken care of."

"I don't think that's going work in this case, Pastor. Trust me, I'm just looking out for you," Tony said.

"I'm not interested in playing games, Detective. Either send me the information or don't. This conversation is over. Have yourself a nice day."

"Does the name Lupe Verdugo ring a bell?" Tony asked.

After a long pause, Jacob said, "Meet me at my estate here in Southlake in two hours. I'll text you the address."

"I will see you there," Tony said.

They both hung up.

Tony pulled into the long driveway and was stopped short by an entry gate. Cherubs playing harps adorned the top of the massive golden barrier. The front gate was framed by tall, beautifully manicured hedges. Tony couldn't see the house from here but he had a pretty good idea of what to expect. He decided he was in the wrong business. Tony reached his hand out of the window to push the button for the intercom.

"Dreyer Residence. Please state your name and the nature of your business," a disembodied voice said.

"Detective Anthony Donolla and I'm here to see the Pastor," Tony replied.

Very well, Detective Donolla, Pastor Jacob is expecting you. Please drive through. There is parking in front of the house."

"Thanks, buddy," Tony said and rolled up his window. The gates began to open and Tony inched the car forward impatiently. He'd only seen places like this on television. He couldn't help but feel a little intimidated but he knew he'd have to shake that feeling to successfully accomplish what he came here to do.

Tony parked his car just off the circular driveway in front of the enormous house. He got out of his car, straightened his clip on tie, and sucked in his gut. He made the sign of the cross and kissed his hand. Tony walked up the path to the front door.

The door was immense but proportionate. A gold knocker in the shape of a cross was almost too high to reach so he opted for the doorbell. The digitally remastered notes to "Ave Maria" echoed behind the door. Tony heard footsteps approaching. When the door opened, Tony felt a blast of cool air and an overwhelming sense of giddiness.

"Detective, please come in," said a man in freshly starched shirt and bow tie. "Pastor Jacob is waiting for you by the pool."

"Damn, I forgot to bring my suit," Tony replied as he stepped through the doorway.

* * *

TONY WAS LED THROUGH THE colossal house by the man he could only assume was the butler. Each room was more extravagant than the last. Some rooms had ceilings 20 feet high, or more. Tony's scuffed, fake black leather oxfords clicked on the swirling Italian marble. They passed through a room that was empty except for a piano placed against one wall and a potted plant by its side. A giant oil painting was mounted just above the piano. A youthful and muscular Pastor Jacob was depicted shirtless; a large wooden cross held in one arm, while a foot pinned down the head of a defeated demon.

They finally made it to the room that led to the pool. The glass doors automatically slid open. Tony stepped out into a tropical oasis like nothing he had ever seen before. There was a crystal clear pool surrounded by palm trees, waterfalls and rock formations with slides built in. Beautiful women sunned themselves on chaise lounges while others frolicked in the water.

"Welcome to 'Empyrean', Detective," a man in a plush red velvet robe said. Pastor Jacob sat at a shaded table on the veranda. He looked older than Tony thought he would. Lights and makeup worked miracles on stage. A very tall, broad shouldered man in a black suit stood next to him. The man had his hands crossed in front of him. His right hand seemed to be trying to hide what remained of his left. "Give us a few minutes, will you, Naldo?" Jacob said. "Have a seat, Detective. Can I get you a drink? The mojitos are second to none. I think you'd like a mojito. Does a mojito sound good, detective? I'll go ahead and get us a couple of mojitos."

"I'll take a whiskey, if that's alright," Tony said.

"Fliss!" Jacob yelled.

A tall, slender Hispanic girl in a white bikini and high heels appeared at the table in seconds.

"Felicity, this is Detective," Jacob paused. "I'm sorry I can't quite remember your last name."

"Just call me Tony."

"Felicity, this is Detective Tony and he wants a whiskey. I'll have another mojito, extra mint, extra rum." Jacob slapped the girl's backside playfully as she turned to walk back to the thatched roof cabana at the far side of the veranda.

Tony couldn't take his eyes off the girl as she walked away. Her skimpy white bikini bottom was swallowed up by her cheeky perfection.

"Let's talk, Detective Tony," Jacob said.

"Just 'Tony' is fine."

"Alright Tony, why are you here? What do you want from me?"

"First of all," Tony said. "How did you get a girl like that to work for you? Holy shit."

"Let's just say her parents owed me a favor. She just turned 17 last month," Jacob said, smirking. "But anyway, what's up, man? What are you trying do here?"

"I think we're both businessmen, am I right? I think I know stuff that would help you, and you can help me in the process. Seem fair?"

"I need to know what the hell you're talking about maybe we can come to an agreement," Jacob responded.

"Your whiskey, señor." Felicity returned with the drinks and set them on the table. Tony's jaw dropped. He shook away the fantasy and continued.

"Your name has come up a few times when it comes to missing people. Most of this shit is like 20 plus years ago. I wouldn't be worried about it too much. There is, however, an eye witness to some things that don't make you look too good. I see a potential scandal, maybe. Nobody wants bad press. You'll probably be fine."

"Are you trying to blackmail me, Detective?" Jacob asked.

"I'm trying to provide a service," Tony said.

"I don't think I'm interested in your services, Detective. I'll have Felicity show you out."

Tony gulped down his whiskey in one swallow and slammed the glass on the table. He leaned in closer to Jacob and looked him in the eyes.

"Listen here, shitbag," Tony whispered loudly. "I'm trying to save your ass, here. You're the number one person of interest at the moment and trust me, they're about to turn your life upside down. They'll dig through everything to find even the smallest thing to justify their efforts. Maybe, you're innocent of this, but I'm pretty goddamned sure you got skeletons for days. They'll probably want to question your hot, little, underage piece of ass over there, too. Does she have a green card? I thought I detected an accent."

"Alright, I get it. You've made your point, Detective," Jacob said.

"I can't get you out of trouble if you're deep in the shit, but I can give you a heads up when things are about to go down. I'll give you updates on how the investigation is going and, more importantly, I can lead things in another direction. Maybe, lose some evidence along the way if the price is right. I'm a very influential man down at headquarters."

"Fliss!" Jacob screamed.

Sensing the urgency, Felicity came running to the table. Tony almost broke character as he watched her bounce across the patio.

"Sí, Pastor Jacob," Felicity said.

"Be a dear, and fetch me my checkbook," Jacob said. "Thanks, Darlin'"

Felicity returned within minutes with the checkbook and then disappeared back behind the cabana bar. Jacob wrote a check and ripped it out of the book. He slid it across the table to Tony. "This'll have to do it."

Tony looked down at the check and fought the urge to shoot his gun in the air and kiss the man. Instead, he calmly folded the check and put it in his shirt pocket. "It'll do. For now. I'll keep you posted."

Tony rose from his chair while Jacob remained seated. "Hey, you need to tell me who that eyewitness is," Jacob said. "I, at least, paid for that much."

Tony patted his chest pocket. "I'll think I'll wait for this to clear first," Tony said. "We'll be in touch. I'll see myself out."

8

QUITMAN, TEXAS
June, 1969

"WHERE'S DADDY, MAMA?" THE LITTLE boy asked. He sat next to his mother on the wooden porch swing that was securely fastened to the ceiling joists of their 1965 Roadliner Dubl-Wide trailer. The view from the front porch was never disappointing. The cover of the piney woods of East Texas had a way of making you feel serenely isolated and alone. If it wasn't for the heat and mosquitos and snakes and absence of running water, it was paradise, lost.

"He's at the church, Jacob," his mother said. "Daddy has to work on his sermon. Now, hush up for a minute and read along with me." She turned the page of her worn, leather bound bible and continued reading aloud.

Jacob listened to his mother read but couldn't help but let his five year old mind wander. It was too hot to pay attention. Jacob wore shorts and a stained white sleeveless undershirt while his mother was dressed in a long sleeved blouse and a skirt that cut off mid ankle. Fortunately for her, the fashions for Pentecostal women kept her covered up. The mosquitos could hardly find a place to land and the bruises on her legs and arms were invisible to anyone she might come in contact. The red handprints around her throat were harder to conceal.

"I want to tell him what I learned today," Jacob said. "Maybe Daddy'll put it in his sermon Sunday."

"Maybe in a little bit, Jacob," his mother said. "For right now, let's read and then you can help me with supper. Okay?"

"Okay, Mama," Jacob said.

The trailer was only a few hundred yards from the Anointed Enlightenment Pentecostal Assembly of God, which was almost halfway between Quitman and Winnsboro. Nestled amid the trees, the tiny church was hardly noticeable to the few cars that passed by on Farm to Market Road 2966. Jacob's father, Isaac Dreyer, would jokingly tell his Sunday flock, "Ya'll better sing louder or God might just forget we're out here in the sticks." That line always got the desired response.

Jacob's mother closed the bible and stopped swinging. Jacob raised his head from her shoulder and looked up at her. "Get your hands washed at the pump out back and come inside to help me put supper on," she said. Jacob reluctantly hopped off the swing and did what he was told.

* * *

"YOU START ON THE POTATOES, Jacob. The peeler's in the top drawer. I'll start chopping carrots. I don't want to see skins all over the floor like last time, okay?"

"Yes, Mama," Jacob replied. He dreaded having stew again. It was way too hot for stew. He didn't really know what stew was supposed to be anyway. It was always just carrots, onions, and potatoes in hot water. She said there was meat in there but he couldn't ever remember getting any.

Jacob helped his mother put the peeled and chopped vegetables in the large cast iron pot on the wood burning stove in the corner of the small kitchen. The stove was ideal for keeping the house warm in the winter and, apparently, for making water soup. Even with all the windows open, the temperature of the kitchen was becoming unbearable and Jacob asked if he could go outside to play.

"You stay within earshot, son," Jacob's mother said. "You hear me? Don't go wandering into the road. Supper'll be ready in about an hour. Daddy should be back by then and you know how he gets. Don't test his patience."

"I won't, Mama. I promise." Jacob kissed her cheek and walked out the front door.

Within about five minutes, Jacob had exhausted all the fun things you could do in a front yard by yourself. He picked up a big stick and swung it around like a sword, he threw some rocks against a tree, and he was now holding a tiny green lizard that was doing its best to avoid his kisses. One quick bite to his bottom lip and the creature was airborne.

He really wished his brother was home. They'd find something fun to do together. Jacob's brother was away at summer bible camp for two weeks over at Lake Quitman. Jacob's Daddy said they could only afford camp for one of them this year and his brother did all his chores on time without being asked, so he got to go. Jacob always felt his brother was Daddy's favorite.

Jacob walked to the mailbox at the edge of the property. He opened it. It was empty. He closed the mailbox and opened it again quickly to see if anything had changed. It hadn't. He looked to the left and saw trees and a lonely stretch of road. He looked right and saw the same except for the tiny white cross of his father's church peeking through the branches. It was so close.

He heard a rustling in the bushes at the perimeter of the yard and quickly ran over to investigate. Jacob's heart raced. He picked up another stick sword and was prepared to slay whatever beast emerged. He couldn't see anything through the bushes but it sounded big. Really big. It could've been a bear or a mountain lion, or worse. Jacob stood about a foot away from where the noise was coming from. He gripped his stick firmly like a caveman wielding a club, and waited for his chance to strike.

A baby armadillo walked out from the shrubs, happily foraging for insects, and paying no attention to the five year old Neanderthal warrior ready to mount its head on his cave wall and use its armor for protection in battle. Jacob dropped his stick and stared. He'd never seen a live one before. He saw a dead one on the side of the road once. Somebody had turned it on its back and put a beer bottle between its legs. Jacob didn't really get it, but it looked funny. He watched the armadillo sniff the ground and prance along the shoulder of the road on its tiny legs. Jacob had to investigate. He knew he wasn't supposed to leave the front yard, but this was for science.

Jacob followed the armadillo as far as he could before it made it's way back into the bushes. He was pretty far from his house now, but not quite out of earshot. The cross from his father's church appeared much larger than it did before. He was about halfway from the church and his house. He really wanted to tell Daddy about all the stuff he learned with Mama today. She read Psalms 137 out loud to him and it was about throwing babies against rocks. He couldn't believe that was in there. His Mama said it had something to do with casting your sins away and how that's pretty important. If his Daddy was preparing a sermon for Sunday, he needed to know this. Jacob decided it was essential he made it to the church.

The marquee sign at the front of the church read, "IF YOU THINK IT'S HOT NOW YOU BETTER COME TO CHURCH SUNDAY - PASTOR ISAAC". The poorly spaced plastic letters were intermittently red and black with no discernible pattern. Jacob walked past the sign, up the two steps, and stood before the double doors. He tried the handle and the door opened.

The church was empty. Jacob walked down the aisle towards the back office where he was pretty sure Daddy would be slumped over a notebook, writing. The office door was closed. Two cups and a half empty bottle of brown liquid were placed on the floor outside the office. Jacob picked up the bottle to see what was inside. It smelled like bad cough syrup. He could hear movement on the other side of the door, like people were exercising or something.

Jacob turned the knob and pushed the door open. A wide, naked, fleshy back, jostled in front of him like a basket of freshly laundered towels hitting the floor in slow motion. A dirty mop head of grey hair bounced in time to the rhythm.

"Daddy?" Jacob whispered. "Are you here?"

Jacob saw his father's head peek out from behind the wall of flesh.

"Jacob, what the hell are you doing here?" Isaac yelled. The grey haired woman turned her head and saw the little boy standing there, wide eyed and confused. She dismounted and grabbed the nearest article of clothing she could find to try to cover herself. She stood up and backed out of the office.

"Get over here boy! It's time for a whoopin' you worthless little shit." Isaac pulled his pants up, fastened the button, and zipped up his fly, before removing his belt. Jacob stood there too frightened to move.

"I just wanted to tell you what I learned today, Daddy."

"Not another word," Isaac said, and grabbed Jacob by the arm and threw him over an office chair.

"Please Daddy, no!," Jacob pleaded.

"What did I tell you about talkin'? You're just stupid aren't you? You're just a stupid little piece of shit. I wanna hear you say it. Tell me how stupid you are."

Jacob's crying prevented him from responding. He sobbed and sputtered as he lay bent over the chair.

The first crack of the belt was always the most painful, and this one was more painful than any other Jacob could remember. "Tell me you son of a bitch! Tell me you're stupid or the next crack will be harder."

"I'm…stupid…Daddy," Jacob was finally able to get out.

"That's right you are. You're Daddy's stupid little embarrassment. You are the biggest disappointment to your Mama and me. We never wanted you. You just showed up and ruined our lives. We'd be better off if it was just your brother. He's the good one." The belt slapped against Jacob's backside again and he squeezed his eyes shut, wishing he was anywhere else.

"You are never gonna amount to nothing you worthless child. Now get out of my sight. You better dry those tears before you go home to Mama. She'll beat you too if she finds you been round here. I bet she told you not to leave the yard. Too stupid to follow instructions, huh? If I hear that you mention one word of what you think you saw here today, I'll kill you, you understand?"

"Yes, sir," Jacob whimpered.

"Now git, before I have to beat you again."

Jacob ran out of the church and down the road. He still had 15 minutes before dinner was ready and he needed to figure out a way to stop crying and to not look like he ever had been. He was going to have a hard time sitting at the table tonight on his bruised and battered backside. He tried to find the humor in his sore butt.

He almost convinced himself everything was okay with a forced a giggle.

* * *

"YOU'RE AWFUL QUIET, SON" JACOB'S mama said. "Did you have fun playing outside?"

Jacob nodded without making eye contact. He noticed there were three more pots on the stove. He didn't think they were expecting company. Maybe mama knew about the other lady Daddy was with.

"Grab one of them pots, Jacob, and help me take it down the hall," his mother said. "I'm gonna have a nice hot bath after dinner and, if you're good, you can take one right after me. The water should still be warm. You'll be all clean and ready for bed."

Jacob grabbed a pot of hot water and followed his mother to the bathroom. She must have been repeating this routine for some time, because the rusty porcelain tub was almost full. The bathroom was steamier than the other rooms in the trailer, which were already steamier than necessary.

"Help me get the table ready, son."

Jacob grabbed some stained, clean placemats from the drawer and set the table. He placed a spoon on the right side on top of a paper napkin. Jacob placed the "Lot" and "Lot's Wife" salt and pepper shakers in the middle of the table. His mama always got a chuckle out of those. She found them at a garage sale a while back near Lake Fork and they just tickled her.

Jacob's father burst through the front door.

"Whatever that boy told you, ain't true. I swear to God," Isaac said. "I was only there to guide her. She had some issues she was working through and I was just guiding her."

"What are you talking about?" Jacob's mom asked. "What woman?"

"Just a lady that needed some help. That's all."

"Dinner is ready. How do you know this woman? What is going on? Is she alright?"

"You're asking a lot of questions right now. I think it might be best if you get dinner served. We can talk about this another time," Isaac said.

"Can you tell me who this woman is?"

Isaac slapped his wife with the back of his hand so forcefully it almost made her fall. "Don't backsass me woman! Now let's just sit down and eat."

She put her hand to her cheek, ladled two bowls of stew, and put them on the table. She backed away from the table. "I think I'll take my bath now while the water is still hot." Her voice was calm yet detached.

"Suit yourself," Isaac said between spoonfuls.

After the bathroom door closed, Isaac stared at Jacob who was quietly working on his own dinner. With stew glistening on his chin and dripping off his lips, he pointed his spoon at Jacob. "You might've kept quiet this time, but I know how you and your mama like to get to gossiping. If I catch wind you been talking to her about anything, you won't be able to sit for a week. You understand?"

Jacob found it hard to imagine his backside being in more pain than it was currently. "Yes, Daddy."

"And don't say nothing to your brother either. He don't need to worry himself about none of this. You'll just go causing more trouble than you need to. You've done enough already."

* * *

"JACOB, GO CHECK ON YOUR mama. She's been in there for damn near an hour now," Isaac said from the tattered green armchair in the living room. "Those dishes aren't going to clean themselves."

"Yes sir." Jacob had already collected the bowls and spoons from the table and put them in the sink. He would have washed them along with the pots but his father wouldn't let him. He always told him it was "woman's work" and he "wasn't about to raise no sissy".

Jacob walked down the narrow wood paneled hallway and stopped at the bathroom door. He put his ear to the door and heard nothing. He knocked timidly, at first. "Mama," he called. No answer. "Mama, Daddy says you need to get out of the tub so you can clean up the kitchen. I helped a little. Mama?"

"For crying out loud, Becky," Isaac yelled as he made his way down the hall. "There's work to be done. Get yourself out of the damn bath." He pushed Jacob away from the bathroom door and tried the knob. It was locked.

Isaac knocked hard on the door and tried the knob again. "Open the door or I'm breaking it down. If I have to buy another one because of you, there will be hell to pay. You hear me, Becky? You don't want this. Trust me."

Jacob stood next to his father. He started to tremble and wanted to cry. He couldn't let his father see the tears welling up in his eyes. He watched as his father reared back and slammed his shoulder into the door. After the second attempt, the door swung open, nearly coming off its hinges.

He had never seen his mother naked before. Her open mouth and nose were barely covered by the red water. A badly bruised arm dangled over the edge of the tub with the fingers pointing at a razor blade nestled in the crimson ooze.

"Hope you're proud of yourself, son," Isaac said to Jacob. "This is what you get when you start poking your nose where it don't belong. Get in the truck. Looks like we got to head into town."

* * *

HE CAREFULLY PLACED THE SYRINGE in the syringe shaped cutout, closed the book, and put it back in its place on the shelf. Sterilization was unnecessary in this line of work. A little contamination never hurt anyone; or perhaps it did, but he couldn't remember anyone complaining about that, specifically.

The last hour had been the most anticipated and most fulfilling of his career, but the best was yet to come. He was loath to keep food from Gabriel and Raphael for so long. They had missed four feedings, but their reward was coming soon. It would be perfect.

Fortunately, he kept the half full syringe of propofol close by during the extraction. His patient slept peacefully while his tongue was being removed but started to rouse while the jagged teeth of the crocodile shears tore into the flesh of his genitals. They probably needed sharpening. Just a small prick, and it was back to business.

The effects of the extra injection of propofol would be wearing off soon. It was time to get into character. He wished he could be there for the initial reaction when his project regained consciousness, but his imagination would have to suffice. He had placed the severed parts on a metal table next to the man on the slab. Gabriel and Raphael were secure in their glass enclosure. It was time for the final act.

He reached for the leather mask from the drawer at the bottom of the bookshelf. He held it in his hands; its vacant eyes stared back at him as he cradled it. He turned it over and widened the opening with his fingers before sliding it down his face. The gentle caress of the mask against his cheeks was a loving embrace. The scent of leather awakened his senses. Lifting the black hood over his head and pulling it down, he was ready.

The bookshelf only needed to be slid a few inches for the hidden stone door to reveal itself. Both were on tracks fitted with small wheels. The stone door brushed against the stone wall and sounded like the unveiling of an ancient sepulcher. He walked through the opening and made his way down a wooden staircase.

It was evident the man on the slab was still unconscious. He wasn't concerned. There were still a few things left to do. While he heated up a square piece of metal attached to a wooden shaft, he noticed the grey cat toying with the captive. He'd leave it be for now, provided it didn't concern itself with Gabriel or Raphael.

He heard the man cough and saw the cat turn its attention to the rats in the glass box on the man's stomach. He couldn't let that cat destroy his grand finale. If that damned cat overturned the box and Gabriel and Raphael got out, and he had to scramble on the floor collecting them, it would ruin everything. This was no time for amateur hour. It had to be perfect. He continued to heat the metal over the open flame.

Suddenly, the man began to scream his best tongueless scream. He jerked in his restraints, but his movement was limited. Unsettled, the cat jumped off his chest and on to the side table. The metal plate was glowing. Everything was in place, perfectly. Showtime!

He turned to the man on the slab and began marching quickly towards him, holding the heated steel plate by its smoking handle. He never broke eye contact as the man craned his neck forward to get a better look. He saw confusion and fear in the man's face, but he wanted terror. Soon enough.

He stopped at the foot of the stone slab and stared at the man for a brief moment before opening the glass lid of the box with his right hand and placing it carefully on the table. He raised the blazing metal square, gripping the handle with both hands in front of his chest. It was only inches from the opening of the box.

Gabriel and Raphael grew agitated. Though he never took his eyes away from the man's face, he could sense their stress and, since "fight" was not an option, "flight" would soon kick in. He hated to scare them this way but he would make sure they were compensated for their roles. They were innocent pawns in this game and he would never let them get hurt.

He started to lower the heated metal to the opening of the glass box. Gabriel and Rafael began scratching and biting at the skin of the exposed stomach. The man's left eye widened as if there was some recognition. He thought he may have detected the slightest semblance of a smile. Unacceptable.

Plunged another inch, and the rats were in a frenzy. They burrowed into the man's flesh with panicky desperation. The glass walls splashed with red, like beets in a blender. There was no need to push the metal any further. Gabriel and Raphael wouldn't cease until the curtain closed.

Just before the man stopped writhing, the grey cat jumped from the side table and onto the floor. The man's severed tongue flopped around comically from its jaws.

* * *

HE HAD TO GO BACK upstairs to fetch his scalpel and pliers. When he came back down, he was relieved to see Gabriel and Raphael were calm now, but, apparently, still hungry. They nibbled away peacefully. They'd need a bath soon. He'd let them have their fun, first.

He inserted his scalpel just below the good left eye of the dead man's face. He needed some mementos to commemorate such a beautiful performance.

9

SOUTH PADRE ISLAND, TEXAS

March, 2003

HIS FACE WAS SO BURNED it hurt to blink. Aaron sat on a stool at the hotel bar nursing a terrible hangover. He stared at his reflection in the mirror. His face was the same color as the Bloody Mary he was sipping. The alcohol was beginning to work its magic and the tomato juice was the first healthy thing he had put in his body in the last four days. Spring break was taking its toll, but he'd power through it if it killed him.

The last thing he remembered, was chugging beer through a funnel while a large group of college students in swimsuits cheered him on. He managed to down four beers in one turn. The crowd screamed their approval and Aaron decided to celebrate with a victory nap. He woke up on the beach several hours later with sand in his crack, looking like a fire truck.

He had gone back to the hotel room to meet up with his friends but they were nowhere to be found. They were most likely across the border in Matamoros shooting dollar tequila shots. He wasn't really in the mood for all that, but he couldn't spend his spring break alone in his room either. He went down to the hotel bar because it was the only place that served alcohol on the island that wasn't crowded. The drinks were way too expensive for students on a budget. Aaron could sit there and enjoy the air conditioning and an adult beverage like a gentleman. He could also see the wet T-shirt contest going on at the pool through the tinted glass.

"Looks like you could use a friend," Aaron heard a voice say behind his right shoulder. He looked up from his Bloody Mary and into the mirror to see if the voice was for him. He was the only one at the bar. Aaron turned his head to answer and found himself suddenly speechless.

She was the most beautiful girl he had ever seen. Her long, shiny, brown locks perfectly framed her flawless sun kissed skin. Her big brown eyes were more intoxicating than anything in his glass and, though he felt unworthy to be staring into them, he couldn't look away. He felt a gentle breeze on his face when her long lashes blinked in slow motion. The aromas of coconut milk and birthday cake were overwhelming. His hangover was gone. He could no longer hear the commotion from the pool. There was only them and nothing else mattered.

"You okay?" the girl said. "Can I join you, or would you prefer to sit here alone with your mouth open?"

Snapping back to reality, Aaron quickly closed his mouth. Fortunately, his current complexion hid his embarrassment, or did it amplify it? The thought of it made him more self conscious.

"No, please sit down. I sorta zoned out there for a second. It's been a rough week. My name's Aaron. I'd love for you to join my company....um, or have company...with you. Join me, please." Aaron made a futile attempt to pull the stool out next to him. He was only able to move it an inch or two from where he was sitting, but she saw it as an invitation, pulled it out herself, and sat down.

"How many of those have you had, Aaron? I'm Heather. Good to meet you."

"Good to meet you too, Heather," Aaron said, trying to mask his goofy smile. "Can I buy you a drink or something?"

"I think I'm all 'drinked' out at the moment," Heather said. "I came in here to get away from all the madness and I saw you sitting there, and I was thinking 'he doesn't look too crazy, maybe I should go talk to him. I've been wrong before. Plus, I couldn't tell how red you were in the mirror. You poor thing. Does it hurt?" Heather put her hand to Aaron's crimson cheek.

"I'll survive, I think," Aaron replied. "I take it you're here for spring break too?" He instantly regretted asking such a stupid question.

"Actually, I'm here researching dolphin husbandry for an upcoming film," Heather said.

"What? Really?" Aaron said.

"No, silly," Heather said, slapping him playfully on the arm. "I'm on spring break like the rest of them. I just got a little tired of some of the girls I came with. They're back in the room now dressing up like sluts. What school do you go to?"

"A&M," Aaron said.

"Ooh, which one?"

"The real one," Aaron replied. "College Station."

"I'm an Aggie too," Heather said.

"That's awesome! I don't remember seeing you around campus."

"It's a big school, Aaron. What's your major?"

"Sociology with an emphasis on criminology and criminal justice."

"Sounds scary," Heather said.

"I want to be a cop," Aaron said.

"I didn't think cops had to go to college." Heather said.

"I want to be a homicide detective. What about you, Heather? What are you studying?"

"English Lit," Heather said.

"That should come in handy," Aaron said, his confidence building.

"I guess I don't know what I want to be when I grow up. I'm just enjoying the journey," Heather said.

They eventually made their way to a small table nestled in the back of the bar. They sipped sodas and talked endlessly about everything and nothing until the bartender finally yelled out, "last call".

"Do you want to go for a walk on the beach, Aaron?"

"I'd love to. Lead the way," Aaron answered.

The beach was almost deserted. They walked by several spring breakers sprawled out in the sand and a girl who was feeding a trashcan like a mother seagull. Parties raged on nearly every balcony and the hotel pools were still full of life, but the beach was all theirs. They walked under the moonlight and looked at the stars. Aaron found the courage to hold Heather's hand.

They stopped for a moment to listen to the surf. They faced each other and Aaron leaned in and kissed Heather gently on the lips.

"I hope this doesn't sound crazy," Aaron said, "but I don't want this to end."

"I don't see any reason it should."

10

ROCHESTER, NEW YORK

November, 1989

"IT'S FREEZING OUT THERE," FRANK Donolla said, shaking the snow off his boots at the front door. "What a day. I hate this freakin' time of year. Hey Babe, what's cookin'? Smells delicious." Frank walked over to Nadine and kissed her on the cheek.

"I'm making your favorite," Nadine said, "Pork chops with spaghetti. There's bread and butter on the table and I'm just working on the salad."

Frank grabbed a handful of Nadine's right buttock and squeezed. "You're the best Dini. I ever tell you that? The best." Frank took the wooden spoon from the spaghetti sauce and put it in his mouth before returning it to the pot. "Squisito! Babe, I think maybe you should just stick with the salad tonight. I'm grabbing more than a handful here and it's not even Thanksgiving yet."

"Stop it, Frank," Nadine said. "You know I'm trying."

Frank walked over to the kitchen table where his son was sitting. "Anthony, what you working on, buddy?"

Anthony looked up from his project, frustrated. "I gotta make this nativity scene diorama with popsicle sticks, but it keeps falling apart and the glue is getting all over me."

"Who's in the basket there, bud?"

"That's baby Jesus. The three wisemen are G.I. Joes, but I didn't have anything small enough for Jesus so I just glued a peanut to a match box and colored in the sides with a marker."

"You're a smart kid," Frank said, ruffling his son's hair. "Now pass the bread."

"Anthony, move all your stuff to the living room and don't get any glue on the coffee table," his mom said. "Wash up. It's time for dinner. How was work, honey? You look exhausted."

Frank Donolla worked as a forklift operator in Rochester for the last 25 years. The warehouse catered to a few large department stores in the tri state area and shipped various goods all over the country. This time of year meant long hours and plenty of overtime. Frank would have happily traded in the time and a half for a 40 hour week, but he'd survive this year just like all the others.

"You're not going to believe this, Babe," Frank started as Anthony made his way back to the table and sat down. "So they canned Lisle last week," Frank continued. "Right before the holidays, the poor bastard. He was having a rough time already. His wife filed for divorce in October. Merry freakin' Christmas, right? Anyway, so they bring this broad in from Schenectady to take his place. Name's Barbie or Barbara or something. Now I gotta report to this woman every day. She shows up today in some sort of power pantsuit like she's one of the boys and starts barking orders. The world's gone mad. She got no business there. Probably gonna paint the bathrooms pink and get rid of the Playboys. Everything's turned upside down. Chicks have forgotten what they're good at now a days. Stick to the basics and everything'll be ok."

"Well, I think it's good that women are finally getting a fair shake," Nadine said. "It's about time. Maybe she'll be a good boss. You never know. I was thinking about getting a part time job at the mall for the holidays. I might be a perfume girl, spritzing every-body that walks by. We can always use the extra cash this time of year and it would be nice to get out of the house. Your mom could watch Anthony."

"No wife of mine is gonna have no job," Frank declared. "You got plenty of stuff around here to keep you busy and if you get bored with cooking and cleaning, try using that treadmill I got you last Christmas. It's not a laundry rack, you know."

"I just thought, maybe I could help out a little too. We could spend more on presents."

"That's your problem, Nadine. Thinking ain't your strong suit. Leave the thinking to the men and you just make sure you don't for-get the recipe for this sauce. It's amazing, Babe. Isn't it, Anthony?"

"It's the best, Mom," Anthony said through a mouthful of noodles.

"Not only that, Dini," Frank said lowering his voice. "I got Christmas covered this year."

"What'd you do, Frank?"

"Let's just say some of the shipments at work didn't get completely checked in. Some of them had torn boxes. You can't ship out things in torn boxes. I got you something nice."

"You shouldn't have, Frank," Nadine said with a smile.

"Anything for you, Babe. Anthony, remember, you gotta always be one step ahead of the game. Don't let these punks get one over on you. That's how they get you. Always beatin' you down to submission. Get what's yours and don't take any flack from no woman. Except your mom. Always listen to your mom."

* * *

SOUTHLAKE, TEXAS

"SERVICE THIS SUNDAY IS GOING to be epic, Naldo," Jacob said. "Goddamned epic. I don't know how I keep coming up with this stuff. They'll be talking about it for months."

"What are you working on, sir?" Naldo said.

"I've been thinking lately, I need to do a sermon on the End Days. All the other guys are doing it. We don't want to be left behind, so to speak." Jacob waited a second for a reaction out of Naldo. He didn't get one. "Alright then. So I figure we put a little scare into 'em. Get 'em all amped up. Shit, people are gonna be more likely to part with their money if they don't think they got too much time left to spend it."

"Ingenious, sir," Naldo said.

"So the last few weeks, in the evenings, I've been out at Paradise Stables in Argyle and I've been learning to ride a bit. I've fallen off more times than I'd like to admit, but, you know, I think I'm starting to get the hang of it."

"I'm not sure I'm following, sir," Naldo said.

"Alright, picture this, Naldo," Jacob said. "The church is pitch black. The sound of thunder comes out of the speakers. We'll do that surround sound thing so it rumbles in the back and then towards the front, or whatever. Quiet at first, and we'll start to turn it up gradually. Throw in a few flashes of lightening here and there. Hell, I'd turn on the sprinklers just for effect if I didn't think it would chase 'em off. Then, the curtain opens, slowly. I come riding out on a white horse wearing a white crown. Me, not the horse. I got a white bow and arrow and three other horses in tow. Epic, man. The Four Horsemen of the goddamned Apocalypse."

"Sounds amazing," Naldo said, "but who will be riding the other horses?"

"You know I don't like to share a stage with anyone, Naldo. It'll just be me, but I'll have the other three horses tied up together so I'll be sort of leading them on stage behind me. The folks at Paradise are letting us rent out a white one, a red one, and a black one. They said we could paint another white one light green provided we use some safe dye that'll wash out real easy. I never seen a green horse but we'll stay true to the scripture. I got Sophie checking on permits. I don't know that we need any, but better to be safe than sorry."

"You seem to have it all figured out," Naldo said.

"It's coming together for sure," Jacob said. "It'll be seen by millions of people around the world. Man, I'm so fired up I can't think straight. I think I want a drink. You want a drink, Naldo?"

"I'm fine, sir," Naldo answered.

Jacob pushed one of the many buttons on his desktop intercom.

"Yes, this is Felicity. How can I help you, Pastor Jacob?"

"I love how that girl says my name," Jacob said to Naldo before pushing the intercom button again. "Tickles me for some reason. So international, you know?" He pushed the button. "Yes, Baby, can I get a mojito? You know how I like it." He took his finger off the button again. "You want anything, Naldo? Coffee? Juice? It might be a long afternoon. I got a sermon to write and I'm gonna need you to pull out your bible and help me."

"A water is fine, thanks."

Jacob pushed the button. "And a water for Naldo, Fliss. Thanks, hun."

"Alright, let's get to work," Jacob said. "Think dark and brooding and throw in a little scary."

"I think I can handle that," Naldo said.

✳ ✳ ✳

SHE HAD MUDDLED MORE MINT than she ever imagined there was mint to muddle. Pastor Jacob loved his mojitos; extra mint, extra rum. Felicity had never heard of mojitos before she came to America. She figured most 17 year old girls probably hadn't. She was fortunate enough to have the opportunity to be here, so she couldn't complain. It wouldn't do any good, anyway.

Felicity had been in Southlake for almost three years now. She remembered the night the black van arrived at her house in Juárez to pick her up. She remembered her mother and father crying; her mother was in hysterics. It must have been so hard for them to see her leave. They knew what was best for her and she knew she would find a way to repay them, somehow. She didn't make much money working for Pastor Jacob, but whatever she made, she put in an envelope and gave it to the Pastor to mail to her parents every week. She didn't really have use for money, anyway. Her room and board was included and she couldn't leave the house until her paperwork came back from immigration. The Pastor was working on all of that for her. Felicity hoped the money she sent her parents would help them start their immigration journey, too.

Felicity was supposed to be going to school, but she couldn't register until her papers came in. Until then, she read everything she could get her hands on; whenever she wasn't cleaning, or cooking, or making mojitos, that is. It didn't take her too long to learn English. The Pastor had given her a few remedial Spanish to English courses and she read them over, several times. The rest of the staff were a big help as well. She probably talked their ears off the first year she was there. Books were limited around the house, but she had read the bible twice and two of Pastor Jacob's books; once was enough for those.

She hadn't spoken to her family since she arrived in Southlake. Her family was so poor they didn't have a phone or much of anything else. They tried to call collect every few months and Pastor Jacob would take the call. She was always too busy to talk, but the Pastor would take down the message and relay it back to her. He didn't like collect calls. They always sent their love and told her that her two brothers and little sister were doing well and that they couldn't wait to be able to come visit soon. Until then, she would send them what she could and try to make them proud.

Felicity placed the mojito and a bottled water on the cocktail tray. "Salad in a glass," the Pastor would say. She never found that funny, but she would fake a giggle and play along. She lifted the tray with her right hand and placed a white envelope in her apron pocket with the other. She walked through the automatic glass doors and made her trek to Pastor Jacob's office.

* * *

"TALK TO DIANE IN PROPS, today, Naldo," Jacob said. "I need a white crown and I want it sparkly. Tell her to bedazzle that shit if she has to. Same for the bow and arrow. We need some sashes or something coming off the other horses to let the audience know what they are. 'Death' is a green horse for some reason, so we got to make it a little scarier. People won't be too scared of a green horse. Have Diane find a skull mask or something to put over it's head. Tell her it's in the budget. We can't get all chintzy on this one."

"I'll call her right after this, sir," Naldo said as he wrote diligently in his notebook.

A knock sounded at the office door. "Pastor Jacob, I have your mojito," Felicity said.

"Well come on in, sweetheart," Jacob answered.

Felicity opened the door with her free hand and walked inside the office. She set the mojito in front of Pastor Jacob and handed the bottled water to Naldo.

Jacob took a sip. "Ahh, salad in a glass. Thanks, baby. You can run along now."

Felicity faked a giggle. "Thank you, sir. I have something I need you to mail to my parents, if that's alright."

"Sure baby, hand it over," Jacob said.

Felicity pulled the envelope out of her apron and placed it on the desk in front of the Pastor.

"I'll get this mailed out first thing tomorrow morning," Jacob said. "By the way, your mom called last week. Said she's trying to knit you some socks. I think they were socks. My Mexican's not so good, but I'll let you know if they show up. Thanks, Fliss. I'll call you if we need anything else."

"Oh, thank you Pastor Jacob," Felicity said as she backed out of the room.

After the door closed, Naldo said, "How long do you think you can keep her in the dark?"

"You know as well as I do, Naldo, her parents didn't pay me back. I told them what was going to happen and they still didn't pay. I treat her good. She'll be fine. Saves her from slinging penny tacos in the streets of Juárez. Some day she'll pay me back for all I done for her. Trust me."

"You know best, sir," Naldo said.

"That's right, Naldo," Jacob said. "Now let's get back to the matter at hand. We got a show to put on." Jacob slid the envelope across the desk towards himself and opened the drawer. He placed the envelope on top of an assortment of pens and notepads and closed the drawer. He paused for a second, then opened the drawer, picked up the envelope, and broke the seal. He removed the two $20 dollar bills and folded them before putting them in his shirt pocket and discarding the empty envelope in the wastepaper basket next to his desk. "Now, where were we?"

Jacob's mobile phone vibrated in his pants pocket as a new text message came through. He pulled out his phone and read the text.

"Naldo, I might need you to take care of something."

✳ ✳ ✳

FRISCO, TEXAS

"I CAN'T BELIEVE PEOPLE WANT to live out here. Where's the action?" Tony said as they drove down FM 423. "I guess there are people who like the peace and quiet, but I think I'd go out of my mind. To each their own."

"After seeing the stuff we see on a daily basis," Aaron said, "I'd take a little peace and quiet any day. Looks like a good place to raise a family. Scott would love it, I'm sure. I'd get him that dog he's been hounding me about. No pun intended. I think a change of scenery might do us good in the next few months."

"Any change with Heather, buddy?" Tony asked.

"No. We're still $250,000 away from the $250,000 goal," Aaron said. "She goes in to surgery to have the tumor removed next week. She might not even survive that. Scott's been asking why Mommy's still sleeping. I don't know what I'm supposed to tell him or if he'd even understand."

"Whatever happens, you know Carol and me are here for you," Tony said. "In fact, I'm willing to offer Carol up, right now. Just take her. She's yours. I'm willing to pay, here." Tony slapped Aaron's leg from the driver's side and chuckled. Aaron appreciated his attempt to lighten the mood and smiled back at him before turning his gaze out the window.

They pulled off the main road just after a sign that read "Saint Anthony of Padua Catholic Church Next Right". They traveled less than a half of a mile down a bumpy dirt road until the small church was visible on the left. They parked next to a white cargo van. The detectives got out of the car and made their way toward the church.

* * *

"BE A DEAR, AND SEE if we can't organize a bit of a food and clothing drive in a week or two," Father Quinn said. "You know how all the computer things work. Maybe, put a blob out on Craig's Book. The orphans could use whatever we can get, and the homeless here in Frisco could use some blankets and food. If you come across a kettle with a handle that's not been glued back in place five times, I might nick that for myself. It'll be our little secret, Sister Sarah." Father Quinn winked.

"I'll take care of it, Father," Sarah said, typing notes on her keyboard.

"We should take the van in for a cleaning. I'm sure it needs one. Maybe, get an oil change," Quinn continued. "Some fellas in town said they'd do it for free or cheap. I think it's one of Bobby's kids. Nice boy. Runs the lube shop there. I think you have the number, don't you?"

"Father Daniel cleans the van himself at least once a week. You couldn't find a crumb. And it just had a tune up, oil change, and 20 point inspection, Father. It's tip top. All the stickers are up to date. They took care of us, for sure."

"Be certain to send them a thank you note, would you, dear?" Quinn said.

"Already sent, Father, and..." The door to the office swung open and two men in cheap suits walked in.

"Can we help you, gentlemen?" Sister Sarah asked.

The dark haired man pulled a badge from his inside jacket pocket. "Fort Worth P.D., ma'am. We're looking for Daniel Verdugo. I'm Detective Anthony Donolla and this is my partner, Detective Aaron Rider. Is he available?"

"What's this about?" Quinn asked.

"We just need to ask him a few questions, Father," Aaron said. "He's not in any trouble. We're just working on a case and we need to get his take on things."

"Daniel's a good boy," Father Quinn added. "He's probably out in the churchyard making sure everything looks nice. He may be in his office out there at the far end of the cemetery. It's just at the back of the church. I'd take you there myself but you could make it there and back before I could get out of this seat. You can't miss it."

"Thank you Father, and thank you Sister for all your help," Aaron said.

The two detectives made their way out of the office and closed the door behind them.

* * *

"AN OFFICE IN THE BACK of a cemetery? Sounds a little spooky, don't you think?" Tony said. They walked around to the back of the church and stood before the gate leading into the churchyard. "Here goes nothing. These places give me the creeps." Tony made the sign of the cross and pushed the gate. It swung open silently.

The officers walked past rows and rows of old headstones. Though many of the dates had been etched more than a century ago, the stones were polished and each gravesite adorned with flowers. As they made their way to the back of the cemetery, the dates became more recent. Some of the plots were likely covered with dirt only weeks, or even days, ago. There were several empty holes awaiting tenants.

"It's the fresh ones that give me the heebie-jeebies the most," Tony said. "Like maybe, they ain't quite all the way dead, know what I mean? If I was out here by myself at night, I swear to God I'd hear scratchin' or some shit. You might need to hold me, Aaron."

"Will you quit, already?," Aaron said. "Out of respect for the dead, can you shut up for a minute? If not for them, maybe for me?"

"Sorry, didn't realize graveyards got you so uptight," Tony said. "I'll back off."

"Remember, we're here to tell a man that we might have some information about the person who killed his mother. We don't know how this is going to go down. Show a little compassion, or at least a little restraint."

"Alright, alright, I get it," Tony said. "Jesus. I'll be good."

They continued walking until they saw a man in a black shirt and pants crouching next to a wheelbarrow full of dirt. He had his back to them. The wheelbarrow sat next to a large stone structure that looked like a mausoleum. Tony remembered seeing some above ground graves like this one when he and Carol vacationed in New Orleans for Jazz Fest a couple of years ago.

"Father Daniel Jesus Verdugo? Is that you, Father?" Aaron asked.

The man in black didn't acknowledge Aaron, and, instead, continued working on whatever gardening project was at hand.

"Yo, Padre!" Tony yelled. "You hear us or what?"

The priest looked back at the officers and pulled out his ear buds. He looked briefly at Aaron and then locked eyes with Tony for, what seemed much longer than appropriate. He swiveled his head back around before standing up and turning to face the officers.

"What can I help you with, gentlemen?" the priest asked.

"We'd like to have a few words with you, Father," Aaron said. "We're with the Fort Worth Police Department and we'd appreciate it if you could talk to us for a bit."

The priest gestured with his left hand. "Step into my office. We can talk there."

* * *

"NICE TATTOO," TONY SAID. "I didn't think you guys were allowed to have those."

Daniel rolled down his sleeves and buttoned his cuffs, covering the ink on his right arm. The detectives sat down on empty paint buckets across from the priest. They were separated by a wooden plank perched on more empty paint buckets in the mausoleum that appeared to have been converted into a work shed and office. Gardening equipment was placed next to filing cabinets and bookshelves.

"James 1:15," Tony said. "What is that, like a bible quote or something?"

"I had it done in college," Father Daniel said. "What can I help you with, officers?"

"I'm Detective Rider and this is Detective Donolla," Aaron said.

"Hey, Aaron," Tony said, "while were here, maybe Father Daniel can say a little prayer for Heather. Couldn't hurt, right?"

"That's okay," Aaron said, "Father, we're just here to ask a few questions if that's alright with you."

"Who is Heather and how can I help?" Daniel asked.

"It's his wife," Tony interrupted. "She's out at Methodist back in Fort Worth. She's in a coma. She needs to have a brain tumor removed."

"That's not why we're here, Father," Aaron said. "We have some information on a cold case that we need to discuss with you and, maybe, get your input on the situation."

"I visit Methodist hospital at least once a week," Daniel said. "I work with the children in the juvenile oncology ward. I would be happy to say a prayer for your wife or stop by her room the next time I'm there."

"She needs all the help she can get," Tony said. Aaron flashed him an angry look. Tony continued, "What? Am I crazy? Heather needs some help. The doctors don't seem to be doing anything for her, and, maybe, Padre over here might do her some good."

"I apologize for my partner right now," Aaron said, looking embarrassed. "This isn't why we're here."

"I can tell these things weigh heavy on your mind, Detective," Daniel said. "Perhaps before we start, I can say a prayer for you and your wife."

"I mean no disrespect, Father," Aaron said, "but, I'm not really a believer. I'm just worried about my son, Scott. I don't know how to tell him his mother only has a few months to live. He's such a good boy. He's only five. He shouldn't have to deal with this. Nobody should have to deal with this." Aaron gritted his teeth and tried to hide his watering eyes, but his flushing face was giving him away.

"The Bible says almost nothing about guardian angels," Father Daniel began, "but I've found when working with dying children or people dealing with the loss of a loved one, bending the words of scripture in the name of comfort and kindness works best. Make sure you let Scott know that his mother will always be with him, watching over him, to care for him, and make sure he is always safe. When he talks to her, she will hear him, and though she may not respond, she is there."

"That sounds nice, Father," Aaron said. "I'll pass that on to my son. I appreciate it."

"I can sense that you are a good man," Daniel continued, "with much love in your heart. Remember, 'guardian angels' come in many forms. Sometimes they appear when you least expect them."

"Kinda like me, huh Father?" Tony interrupted. "I'll take care of him. Now if we can only find a guardian angel with an extra $250,000 lying around, Aaron's wife might get the medical treatment she deserves."

Father Daniel looked at Tony for a moment then turned to Aaron. "I don't understand," Daniel said.

"There's an experimental cancer treatment that I'll never be able to afford," Aaron said. "We should really discuss what we came her to discuss. I'm sorry we've wasted this much of your time already, Father."

"Psalm 34:15 says, 'The eyes of the Lord are on the righteous and His ears are attentive to their cry,'" Daniel said. "Be strong and God will reveal his plan for you and your family."

"Thank you again, Father," Aaron said.

"Hey, I go to church every Sunday, Father," Tony said. "I'll be sure to say a prayer for them too. I grew up Catholic, you know."

Father Daniel ignored Tony's statement and continued to look into Aaron's eyes. "Now, how can I help you, Detective?"

"We don't have much to go on so far, Father," Aaron said. "There are some people who have recently gone missing throughout the Dallas Fort Worth Metroplex. We have done a little digging and there could possibly be a connection with your mother's disappearance back in June of 1995. Was your mother's name Maria Guadalupe Verdugo?"

"That's correct," Daniel said. "What information do you have?"

"It's really all speculation at this point," Aaron said. "We just need to find out if you remember anything about the night she disappeared."

"I was very young when it happened," Daniel said. "I must have been about your son's age. It's all a bit of a blur, I'm afraid."

"Just tell us what you think you saw, if you saw anything," Tony said.

"Anything you can recall will help," Aaron said. "We're sorry to to dredge up painful memories."

"I remember we went on a long bus ride from El Paso to Dallas. I thought we were on vacation but the place we were staying in wasn't very nice. We never left the motel room. We were supposed to have pizza, I remember that. I went to go wash up for dinner and when I came out of the bathroom..," Daniel started breathing heavily.

"Take your time," Aaron said. "It's alright. I know it hurts."

"I came out of the bathroom," Daniel continued, "and this man in a black suit was choking her. Her feet were off the ground. I couldn't do anything. He just kept choking her. She went limp and he twisted her neck and threw her on the ground. I think she was dead. I couldn't help her. I didn't do anything."

"Do you remember what he looked like?" Aaron asked.

"No," Daniel said. "He was a big man dressed in black. That's all I remember."

"Was there anything else that stood out about this man? Any scars or tattoos?" Aaron pressed.

Father Daniel closed his eyes tightly. A few seconds later he blurted out, "One of his hands was a claw. It was really disfigured." Sweat was forming on Daniel's forehead and he was breathing deeply.

Naldo, Tony thought.

"That's all I remember," Daniel said. "I woke up in an orphanage. The cops came to talk to me and I couldn't tell them anything. I couldn't bring myself to speak. I had so much to tell them and I couldn't say anything! Do you know who did this to my mother?"

"We're are just gathering information at the moment," Aaron said. "We will update you with any new information. We appreciate your time, Father Daniel."

"There's a good chance that none of this is even related," Tony added. "We'll keep you posted, Padre."

Tony and Aaron rose from their respective paint buckets and made their way out of the office. It was apparent the priest would need a few more minutes to absorb the information. He remained hunched over his "desk" and said nothing as they left.

* * *

"I'LL DRIVE," AARON SAID AS they approached the car. "Man, that got pretty intense. Poor guy. We have to find his mom's killer."

Tony threw Aaron the keys and said, "You really think these missing people got anything to do with what happened to that guy's mom in '95? Seems like a bit of a stretch to me. None of the new missing people have been women so far. It was so long ago. I'm telling you, Aaron, Dreyer's not a killer. The whole thing is most likely just a weird coincidence. The delivery guy at the pizza place probably killed his mom and stole the pizza. I think we just spent an afternoon making some guy really sad."

"Well even if it's an isolated case, I think we should help him. He seemed to want to help us," Aaron said.

"Yeah, help you, more like," Tony said. "He took a real shine to you. It was like he wasn't even listening to a word I said. I'm the religious one here. You're the godless heathen, no offense."

"It's kinda like when a dog can tell who's friendly and who's a piece of shit just by sniffing at you," Aaron said. "'Religious one', my ass."

They pulled out of the church parking lot and bounced their way down the dirt road. Tony pulled out his phone and began to type a message with his thumbs.

"Eye Witness = Daniel Jesus Verdugo. More info later :-)" Tony hit "send" on his phone.

Father Daniel put his hands on his knees and forced himself to stand and face the rest of his day. There was work still left to do. With his eyes closed, he stretched his back and rotated his neck a half circle to the left and then to the right. He put one hand on top of the other, squeezed tightly, then switched. The sound of cracking knuckles reverberated off the walls within the confines of the mausoleum office. He pushed his arms forward with fingers inter-locked until he could push no further, then dropped them by his side. Daniel forcefully exhaled and opened his eyes.

He walked through the doorway and into the churchyard. Staring out into the rows of headstones, he started to feel at peace, once again. Daniel preferred to have complete control over his thoughts. He had spent years storing most of the harsh memo-ries of his childhood under layers of scripture and goodwill. This momentary glimpse into the dark corners of his psyche was more than he cared to recollect. He decided it might be best to have a talk with Father Quinn.

As he began his walk toward the church, he noticed a small commotion at the foot of a tall box elder tree near the hedges that lined the perimeter of the cemetery. A cat had found something very interesting just under the hedges, while remaining completely oblivious to the desperate chirps of a small red bird that continued to execute unsuccessful aerial attacks.

Father Daniel moved in for a closer look. Up in the lower branches of the tree, a beige and red cardinal displayed her discon-tent with the beating of her wings and a series of loud calls to her mate. She perched on the branch close to her nest that contained her two chicks; necks stretched and beaks wide open. Her deeper red companion reported to her periodically between dives. The cat carried on about it's business, unmoved by the frenzy above.

After closer inspection, Daniel saw what piqued the cat's curiosity. It was mauling a third chick that must have fallen from the nest. It scratched at the baby bird, picked it up in its jaws only to drop it to the ground and repeat the process. The cat swatted at the baby and sent it tumbling a few inches before swatting it back with the other paw. It toyed with its innocent prey with no intention to feed; just to inflict pain for its own enjoyment. The chick wriggled on the ground, opening and closing its beak in silent screams.

Daniel reached down and grabbed the cat by the scruff, its claws still lashing out at the chick that now lay motionless on the ground. He tucked the cat under his left arm and looked down at the baby bird to assess the damage. Deep wounds covered its tiny body, a leg was missing, a featherless wing held on by only sinew. Ants started to crawl over the delicate pink skin, piercing it with their pincers, preparing to feast. The chick started to twitch again from the stings of the insect assault.

Father Daniel mercifully brought his foot down and flattened the baby bird. The red cardinal returned to the nest and perched next to his mate. Daniel continued his walk to the church holding the cat under his arm. He stroked the top of its head. He could hear and feel the cat purring.

The purring was interrupted by the sound of small neck bones breaking. The cat's head was forcibly twisted one half rotation and it's wide vacant eyes stared back at him before slowly closing halfway. Without missing a step, Father Daniel tossed the grey cat's lifeless carcass into an open grave.

11

DALLAS, TEXAS

October, 2012

DANIEL HAD ABOUT AN HOUR before his Krav Maga class. By volunteering his time helping the younger students as well as his janitorial contributions, Daniel was able to afford to get his black belt in Karate, his purple belt in Capoeira, and his 1st kyu white belt in Aikido. Krav Maga was his next challenge. He found the discipline calmed him and kept him focussed.

He had already finished college and received a bachelor's degree in Theology with a minor in Medieval Studies and was now attending seminary. He was leaving a lecture about The Inquisition in his History of Doctrine class and was on his way to help pass out sandwiches to the homeless at a nearby mission that was close to his Krav Maga class. He backed the white cargo van down an alley near the mission and parked it as close to the wall as possible..

Daniel got out of the van and heard a woman screaming at the far end of the alley. She appeared to be screaming at a tall man in a black leather jacket who was holding her tightly by the wrist. When she tried to pull away, the man punched her square in the face, dropping her to the cement. Daniel got back in the van.

He turned the ignition and slammed it in reverse. Daniel sped backwards down the alley until he was only a few yards from the scene. He looked in the rearview mirror before opening the door. The man in the black jacket looked terrified. Daniel got out and stared into the man's eyes.

"You the cops, or what?" the man asked.

"Let go of her, and we'll talk," Daniel said calmly. The woman looked up at Daniel from the street. She was crying and blood spewed from her busted nose.

"This doesn't concern you, man. Get back in your van and get up outta here. This won't end good for you. For real."

"Help me," the woman said between sobs.

"Shut up, bitch!" the man yelled. "Don't be playing me like that. You know what you owe me."

"Let her go, and we'll talk," Daniel said. "Man to man."

The man let go of her wrist. "I am getting tired of this shit, man." He looked down at the woman. "I don't know where you think your gonna hide. I know where you stay at, Shontelle. This ain't over between us."

"Get as far from here as possible," Daniel said. "Get out of here now. Get to the mission down the street a ways and to the right. They'll make sure you get the medical attention you need. Go!" The woman grabbed her purse and scrambled to her feet. Daniel could hear the clicking of her purple stilettos echo off the alley walls behind him.

"I won't forget this, Shontelle. I'll see you tonight. Believe that," he turned to Daniel. "Now what the fuck is your problem man? Don't do something you're going to regret."

"You can't treat people that way. You have to give respect in order to get respect," Daniel said.

"You here to give me a manners lecture? Dude, I am done with this. You fixin' to piss me the hell off." The man reached into the waistband of his jeans and pulled out a butterfly knife. He deftly flipped it around in his hand and pointed the exposed blade at Daniel. "What you gonna do n…"

Daniel struck him in the throat with a quick chop. The man dropped his knife and grabbed at his neck, coughing and gasping for air. Daniel walked behind him and put his arms around his head and neck and squeezed until the man slumped over, unconscious.

Daniel unlocked the back doors of the van, picked up the knife, grabbed the man, and heaved him inside. Using a garden hose, some weed eater line, and a few loose bungee cords, he was able to hog tie the man securely. When he began to stir, Daniel stuffed a dirty rag in his mouth and wrapped another bungee cord around his head to keep the rag in place.

He pulled out of the alleyway and took a left. Daniel was going to have to skip his Krav Maga class this evening.

"You're home earlier than expected, Daniel," Father Quinn said, looking up from his book. He took a sip from his teacup. "Everything alright?"

"Yes, Father. I picked something up in town to work on in the churchyard. I'll probably be at it for the next few hours and then I have to study. Don't wait up."

"Very well, son," Father Quinn said. "You work so hard. I'm proud of you, you know?"

"Have to stay busy. 'Idle hands', right, Father? I'm going to get started. That manure won't unload itself. It's probably already stinking up the van."

"Don't work too hard, enjoy yourself from time to time."

"I think I will, Father."

It was difficult lifting the man through the hidden doorway behind the bookshelf in the mausoleum. His squirming stopped after his fall down the wooden stairway. He lay at the bottom, groaning, while Daniel slid the door closed.

Daniel had a few ropes and chains he had collected over the years. He needed to get the man tied to the wall without giving him too much freedom to move. Any mistake here could prove disastrous. This was his place to get away from the rest of the world. It wasn't equipped to store prisoners. Not yet.

After more than an hour of tying ropes and chains to heavier objects in the room, Daniel had managed to restrain the man in a standing position. He pulled out the butterfly knife he retrieved earlier and cut off the man's jacket and shirt. The man tried to scream during the whole process, but the rag in his mouth muffled his pleas. From the looks of the bumps and bruises on his arms and shoulders, the trip down the stairs did more than stop him squirming. Daniel noticed a bone unnaturally pushing at the skin of the man's left forearm.

During his time in college, Daniel had become fascinated with the history of medieval torture. He made it a hobby to try and recreate some of the smaller devices with items he found at yard sales and hardware stores. His first project was The Heretic's Fork that he fashioned from two barbecue forks and an old dog collar. The finished instrument consisted of the metal ends of two forks set against each other, end to end; one penetrating the flesh under the chin and, the other, piercing the victim's sternum. The fork ends were separated by a leather collar that wrapped around the Adam's apple. The victim was forced to look upwards to avoid impaling themselves on the sharp tines. The collar added extra discomfort, making it difficult to swallow the saliva that would collect in the mouth. Daniel was eager to see the fruits of his labor.

After putting every implement in place, Daniel removed the bungee cord and pulled the rag from the man's mouth. Looking at the ceiling, the man coughed while spittle sputtered out of his mouth and ran down his cheeks.

"Why are you doing this?" the man asked frantically. His voice was raspy and desperate.

"The righteous shall rejoice when he seeth the vengeance: he shall wash his feet in the blood of the wicked."

"You're crazy man! I didn't do nothing. She had it coming to her. Please! She's just a whore, man." He paused before whispering, "Like your mama."

Daniel grabbed the man by the back of his head before violently pulling it forward toward his chest. The sharpened tines of the fork dug into his sternum and into the soft flesh of his chin, then up through his tongue and into the roof of his mouth. The man wailed in agony. Daniel grabbed his head and repeated the maneuver. Then again. And again. And again.

Warmth coursed through Daniel's veins as he gazed upon the man's bloody, lifeless face. A sense of serenity and purpose overtook him. He smiled. Daniel was disappointed with his haste, but patience was a virtue he would master in time.

* * *

FORT WORTH, TEXAS

"I APPRECIATE YOU GUYS SHOWING up so late on a Saturday night," Chief Draeger said, "but there's no rest for the weary, am I right?"

"It's not even Saturday night anymore, Chief," Tony said. "I was at home about to go to bed with my wife and I get called into work. Jesus, tonight was date night. It was gonna be perfect. She had already taken three sleeping pills. She don't even move after that. I was gonna sleep like a baby."

"What's the urgency, Chief?" Aaron said. "I had to get an emergency babysitter. That's going to cost me double. What's up?"

"You think I wanna be here looking at your ugly mugs?" Draeger said. "We got some new information on the missing persons case and I think it may be time sensitive. Strike while the iron's hot."

"I don't know if it's too late, Chief, or too early, for your whimsical banter," Tony said. "Just spill it."

"I read your reports on the meeting with the priest," Draeger said. "Not exactly enough for a full blown investigation. I still don't trust that Dreyer guy, but we'll come back to that. I'm sure he's got something to do with those folks that went missing out in West Texas and New Mexico."

"He's a good man, Chief," Tony said, "me and the missus go see him every week. He's a stand up guy."

"For now, I'm not worried about Dreyer, or your opinion, Donolla," Draeger said. "We have some interesting information about that little church you went to visit out in Frisco."

"What are you saying, Chief?" Aaron asked.

"There are about 14 people missing now, and we can see that at least eight of them have some connection with that church. Either they went there, know somebody who goes there, or they're just people that are missing and they're from Frisco or real close by. That guy in the hospital you fellas went to visit, he has a stepson that goes to Sunday School there. Seems like a bit too much of a coincidence, don't you think?" Draeger continued, "I got a hunch that our killer is either from Frisco or he doesn't much care for the people that are. And I'd bet dollars to donuts, he goes to that church."

"So, why are we here at 3:30 in the morning talking about this?" Tony asked.

"Mass will start in a few hours," Draeger said. "I need you boys to get to that church before it starts and talk to the priest. Take the list of missing people with you and see if he recognizes any of the names. If he does, see if he can tell you anything about them that might help the case. Maybe, he knows who might want to hurt them. I'm gonna need you guys to sit through mass and see if anyone seems a little off. I'm sure Father Daniel there could be a big help to the investigation. He shouldn't have a problem cooperating. Let him know we haven't given up on finding his mom's killer."

"I've never been up this early for church, Chief," Tony said.

"You boys go grab some coffee and maybe some breakfast," Draeger said. "Mass starts at 9. Get there an hour or two before that so you can talk to Father Daniel. We don't need to have to add any more folks to our missing person list. Make me proud, fellas."

"We always do, Chief," Tony said.

"Yeah, what he said," Aaron yawned.

* * *

"THANKS SWEETHEART," TONY SAID AS the waitress poured him another cup of coffee. "Do you think I can get some jelly for the toast and a little more syrup?"

"Coming right up, hun."

"Thanks Bonnie. You're a real peach" Tony said and continued to work on the scrambled eggs and sausage portion of his breakfast.

"It's not even 5:00 in the morning," Aaron said, "how can you be shoveling that much food into your face?"

"Most important meal of the day," Tony said through a mouthful.

"If that's the only one you have," Aaron said sipping his black coffee. "I don't want to have to wake you up during the interrogation."

"I'll be in a food coma until noon, probably," Tony joked and then realized his poor choice of words. "You know what I mean. I'll be tired. Sorry. I'll just double the coffee. It'll be fine. I'm awake. I'm good. Not even sleepy."

"Take it easy, man," Aaron said. "It's okay. You don't have to walk on eggshells. Or eat 'em. We're good."

"Thanks," Tony said. "You think we're gonna find this killer abductor person at the church service this morning?"

"Probably not, but I think we'll get closer to figuring it out. Father Daniel will probably give us some info we can use."

"I told you Jacob Dreyer didn't have anything to do with this," Tony said. "He's one of the good ones."

"I don't imagine he's gonna be the killer we're looking for at the church this morning, but he's not out of the woods yet," Aaron said. "I have a feeling there's going to be an investigation. I don't think any of those guys are on the straight and narrow."

"Is there anything else I can get you, gentlemen?" Bonnie asked, placing the check on the table.

"I think we're good, Bonnie. You've been a doll. Thank you," Tony said, grabbing the bill. "I got this one, buddy." They both stood up from the table and Tony threw four dollar bills on the table.

"I had a coffee," Aaron said. "Just coffee. I appreciate the generosity. Some day I hope to be able to return the favor."

"It's time to go to church," Tony said, following closely behind Aaron. Tony reached back and plucked two dollars off the table and put them back in his pocket.

* * *

FRISCO, TEXAS

THIS WAS HIS FAVORITE TIME. People came to mass at 9:00 on Sunday mornings, but Daniel found the hours between 2:00 a.m. and 4:00 a.m., ideal for God's work. It was time to unveil his latest masterpiece. He painstakingly handcrafted all of his implements. He checked the ropes and pulleys. Nothing could be left to chance. They worked perfectly.

During seminary, Daniel was enthralled by stories of the Inquisition. It was only briefly discussed in school, though he spent many hours studying the 700 years of sinner accountability. Teeth for teeth and eyes for eyes. Confessions were worthless these days, but down here, people were certain to spill their guts.

Father Quinn had done his best to rescue Daniel from Saint Mary's Children's Home after the incident with Father Doyle. There were a lot of hoops to jump through in order for him to stay with the priest, but Father Quinn tried to jump quickly through as many as possible. Quinn was eventually able to convince the orphanage and the church that Daniel's presence in Frisco was invaluable and, after several years, they finally gave in. He had taken Daniel under his wing and mentored him. Quinn helped him through school and, in turn, Daniel took care of the cemetery and anything else that needed to be done.

At age 13, Daniel began excavating. He needed a place to escape. A place to quell the demons. A place to think. Thankfully, there was enough donated second hand machinery around for him to begin his underground getaway. He started off small. Just a tiny room where he could read his books by firelight. The lair beneath the mausoleum where he currently stood had been a work in progress for many years.

The mausoleum had been there for nearly a century. A rich oil tycoon from Beaumont had family in Frisco and wanted to spend eternity where his loved ones could easily visit. He had the mausoleum crafted in Houston and shipped to Frisco in 1921. In 1927, a rusty nail punched through the sole of his work boot during a site visit. His locked jaw and toothy smile were the only things the papers cared to report. "So peaceful looking". His family decided to have him cremated immediately to avoid a media spectacle. Three family members went to his funeral. The mausoleum remained vacant.

Everything was in place. The cargo van had been lined with plastic and the pulleys were freshly oiled. Daniel wiped a damp cloth over the metal pyramid fixed to the top off the wooden fence post that was secured firmly to the floor. Two weeks of the damp cloth treatment, ensured there was just enough rust to make a point. Any more, would be obscene. The Judas Cradle was complete. All that was left, was to suspend the unwitting penitent from the ropes over the top of the metal tip, then lower his naked bottom half onto the pointed "seat". It would fit into place, though, snugly at first. The two 35 pound weights that would be attached at the hips, would make sure the rusty metal spike would be tickling his pancreas by lunchtime.

The man who was to meet his fate on the Judas Cradle was an unsuspected bonus. Two weeks prior, Daniel had persuaded an avid child pornography collector to give up the name of his supplier. He was reluctant at first, but after a few cranks of the handle on the head crusher, the man became very talkative; probably, with the hopes of freedom and forgiveness for being so cooperative. After Daniel was certain the man had told the truth, the handle of the head crusher was cranked rapidly forcing the top of the man's skull into his jaw. The effect was surprisingly similar to a junkyard compactor; instead of shattering headlights, eyes popped out of crushed sockets; instead of a mangled grill, the lower jaw cracked its way through the upper. The man grinned like a cartoon sailor. Daniel regretted not having a mirror in place, or a can of spinach.

Daniel had been studying the supplier's routine for the last week and a half. He lived alone out in Krugerville; just under a half an hour away. Without a social life, he went to bed by 10:00 pm. He would be fast asleep by now, and Daniel planned on taking full advantage of that.

Daniel kept the torches lit and made his way through the limestone hallways of his underground labyrinth. He climbed the wooden staircase and slid the stone door on its wheels and stepped through the opening. He slid the bookcase closed and stood in front of it. He only needed a few more items. Daniel opened a small cooler next to the bookcase and pulled out a vial labeled "Propofol" that the hospital had, unknowingly, donated to him for his work with terminal children. He took a book off the shelf, opened it, and grabbed the syringe that was nestled in its nook between the pages. Daniel filled the syringe and flicked it gently, carefully removing any bubbles. While an air embolism may provide a swifter result, it lacked panache. He placed the full syringe in his shirt pocket. The only item left was his black leather mask. He bent over to open the bottom drawer.

With a violent crack to the base of his skull, Daniel's head smashed into the bookcase. His face slid down the shelves as his knees buckled under his weight. Blurriness quickly melted into blackness.

* * *

"WE'RE PROBABLY GONNA FREAK HIM out," Tony said. "Do priests sleep in? It's 5:30 in the morning for Christ's sake," he paused. "Maybe not the best choice of words, considering. What, are we supposed to walk up to him in the graveyard doin' yoga? 'Hey Father, we think you got a murderer in your church. We're here to observe. Just act like we aint here'. Yeah, right."

"You never shut up, do you?" Aaron said. "How much coffee did you have?"

"Bonnie hooked a brother up. What can I say? I'm feeling on point."

"Just tone it down a bit," Aaron said. "This is serious stuff and it's way too early."

"Turn your brights off, dick!" Tony yelled, as a large black SUV sped by them on the narrow dirt road. "Sorry man, that guy blinded me. You saw that, right? Guy almost ran me off the road. Who needs to go that freakin' fast on a Sunday morning on a road like this? His suspension's gonna be shot."

They pulled into the parking lot. A light was on in the rectory.

"I guess they don't sleep in," Tony remarked. "You think they got a doorbell?"

Aaron and Tony got out of the car and made their way to the church rectory. They arrived at the door and knocked lightly. No answer. Tony knocked a little harder. The door still wasn't answered but a low moan could be heard on the other side. Aaron and Tony shot a look at each other.

"This is the police! Is everyone ok?" Tony said. The moaning grew louder.

"Can you open the door?" Aaron asked.

"We're coming in!" Tony yelled. "Back away from the door!" Tony reared back and lifted a leg to kick the door down. Aaron put his arm up to stop him and tried the knob. It opened effortlessly.

With firearms drawn, the detectives burst through the door. The old priest was curled up on the floor. Dried blood was caked on his forehead and around his nostrils. His eyes were almost sealed shut from the swelling of his broken nose. He rocked back and forth on the floor, wailing in agony.

"Are you alright, Father?" Aaron asked. "Father, can you hear me?" No response. "Dispatch we need an ambulance," Aaron said into his two-way radio, "to Saint Anthony's church in Frisco. I can't remember the address. Get them here quick!"

"EMS is on the way," dispatch responded.

Tony cautiously opened the door at the back of the room and peered inside. The light was on and he noticed movement in the far right corner of the bedroom. Someone was crouched in the darkness behind one of the beds.

"Get your hands up now!" Tony screamed. "I see you there you little shit. Hands up or I'll kill you, I swear I will. Don't try me. Get 'em up now!" Aaron ran over to assist his partner.

A small boy stood up from the shadows of the corner. He was shaking and crying.

"Tony, it's a little kid," Aaron said.

"You think I can't see that now?" Tony said. "I got eyes too, you know. A few seconds ago it could have been the guy who roughed up the priest here. But hey, thanks for clearing that up for me. It's just a little kid. Good. Thanks."

"Are you hurt?" Aaron called over to the boy. The boy shook his head. Aaron returned his concern to the old priest.

"Come over here, kid," Tony said. "We're the police. We're here to help. Sorry if I shook you up there. Everything's okay now, okay?"

The child approached Tony sheepishly. "Hey buddy, you alright? What's your name, kid?"

"Adam," the boy said, looking up at Tony with big brown eyes.

"Well, good to meet you, Adam. I'm Detective Donolla and this is my partner, Detective Rider. You can call me Tony if it's easier for you to remember. Now, did you see who did this to the Father here?"

"No," Adam said.

"What did you see, Adam?" Tony asked. "Can you tell us why you're here and why you were hiding behind the bed?"

"I was in the other part," Adam started, "and I was sleeping, and a car came and I woke up. I looked outside the window and I saw a big man and I saw big black car. I got scared and I went to go sleep again, but it didn't work."

"How did you get in here, Adam?" Tony asked.

"I'm not allowed to go outside at night, but I heard more stuff, so I did," Adam said, looking at the floor. "I watched the man put a big thing in the car and then he drove away real fast. Then I heard noises over here and crying and I came here. When I went in the room I saw Father Quinn on the ground and I didn't know what I was supposed to do," Adam started crying. "He didn't talk to me and he kept hurting real bad. Then, I heard more stuff outside and so I wanted to hide and then you walked in and wanted to shoot me."

"Yeah, sorry about that, kid," Tony said. "Old habits, you know. Now, do you remember anything about the man or the car, or anything else you can think of?"

"He was big and scary," Adam said. "I remember the thing on the back of the car."

"I don't think I know what you mean, but you're doing great, Adam," Tony reassured.

"That thing that has letters and numbers sometimes."

"The license plate?"

"I think so," Adam said. "It had a 'C', 'H', and a 'Z' and a 'N', and a number '1' on it. I think that was all of them."

Without much faith, Tony called the license plate into dispatch. "You've been such a big help, buddy. You're doing so good." Tony tousled Adam's hair.

"The son of a bitch woke me up and punched me in the face," Father Quinn growled from the floor.

"You're conscious," Aaron said, surprised.

"Of course I am," Quinn replied. "I've seen worse than the likes of him. Sorry for the colorful language, but he really got my goat."

"An ambulance is on it's way, Father," Aaron said.

"I'll be fine," Quinn said. "I'm worried about Daniel. He kept asking where Daniel was. I was half asleep. I put my glasses on and saw he wasn't in his bed. I must have said he was most likely in the cemetery, I suppose. I'm not sure what I said, really, but he smacked me around a few more times and that's all I can recall at the moment."

"Can you describe him at all? Any details?" Aaron asked.

"Huge Hispanic fella," Quinn said. "One of his hands looked like a foot. Find Daniel. Make sure he's alright. Please. Check the cemetery. He'd be there if he was anywhere."

"Adam," Tony said, "I need you to be a big boy and look after Father Quinn here. Do you understand?"

"Yes."

"The ambulance is almost here, okay? Everything is going to be fine," Tony reassured.

Tony and Aaron left the church and hurried over to the cemetery to investigate.

* * *

"THE LICENSE PLATE NUMBER 'C', 'H', 'Z', 'N', '1'," dispatch interrupted, "are vanity plates registered to Jacob Dreyer of Southlake."

"'Chosen One', of course," Tony said to Aaron, shaking his head. "Arrogant prick." Tony pushed the button on his radio, "10-4."

"I'm looking up the address now," dispatch continued. "I should have that location in just a moment. It's unlisted, but give me a second."

"I think we know where we need to go," Tony responded, then saw the puzzled look that Aaron shot him. "But if you have a physical address, that would be perfect."

They walked quickly and cautiously through the graveyard. They weren't sure who they were up against and every tombstone was a potential hiding place.

"It's like there's a fucking zombie with a gun behind every one of these things," Tony said quietly. "I am freaking out right now, bro."

Aaron looked back at Tony with a look that begged him to shut up.

"You think we're gonna find a dead priest?" Tony whispered as they crept up to the mausoleum. Aaron put his finger to his lips, hoping Tony would get the hint. A light was on inside.

Aaron motioned to Tony for him to go behind the mausoleum and stand on the other side of the doorway. Tony walked around the backside and stood waiting for Aaron's cue. Both, had their firearms unholstered and in temple index position.

Aaron nodded to Tony and they sprang into action. With guns drawn, they jumped into the doorway. They saw only the empty office. Everything was quiet.

They holstered their guns for the moment, but kept the top flaps unfastened, just in case.

"Do you think they took him?" Tony asked Aaron.

"He doesn't seem to be here," Aaron replied. "Let's take a look around."

At first glance, everything was in the same place as it had been before. Paint cans and wooden planks were untouched. Upon further inspection, Aaron discovered a small open cooler next to the bookcase and a book that had most likely fallen off a shelf. The cooler contained four vials; three empty, one full. The book had pages cut out revealing a hidden compartment.

"'Propofol,'" Aaron said, holding up an empty vial. "This book has a hole in it. Looks like something was hidden in there. I don't think it was a crucifix."

"What is going on right now?" Tony said. "What did we just walk into, buddy?"

Aaron noticed some blood stains at the bottom of the bookshelf and a few sprays of blood spatter on the floor and wall. "Something went down here," Aaron said.

Aaron looked closer at the bookcase. It appeared to be on tiny wheels. He jostled it to the right, and with little effort, it began to slide. As the bookcase shifted, a stone doorway opened.

A strong stench of decay blasted into the small space where the detectives were standing. They were both quick to put a hand over their mouths and noses. Aaron and Tony looked down a wooden staircase into a fire lit room. They stood there for a moment before sliding the bookcase back.

"We've got to get to Jacob Dreyer," Aaron said. "We need to find Father Daniel. Get a crime scene unit here as quick as possible."

"Dispatch," Tony said. "Shit has hit the fan at Saint Anthony's Church in Frisco, get a CS unit here, now. Back of the cemetery. There is a room underneath a tomb that smells like death. It has torches. Slide the bookcase. It's a secret room. Something is dead down there. We don't fully know the potential risk of the situation. Send the most qualified cops. We have no perps yet. We gotta pursue a lead. Time sensitive. Don't send rookies."

"10-4 detective," dispatch answered. "Officers have been dispatched."

Tony pulled out his phone and sent a text message.

* * *

"I'LL DRIVE," TONY SAID. "IT'S only about 30 minutes away. We'll get there in 15." There was an ambulance parked in the parking lot of the church. The lights were flashing but the sirens were off.

"Where are we headed?" Aaron asked. "The house or the church?"

"Let's try the house first," Tony said. "It's close to the church," he paused, "I think. It probably is. I mean, Southlake's not that big, right? It should be close. It will be crazy if we have to meet him at the church. It's a madhouse there on Sundays. But, I guess we'll figure it out soon enough."

* * *

SOUTHLAKE, TEXAS

IF SHE COMPLETED ALL HER chores early enough, she could spend the morning and most of the afternoon reading. Pastor Jacob would want lunch and a beverage after service, as usual, but she was an expert at mojitos and she didn't have to make lunch, she just had to carry it in on a tray. Felicity dusted and wiped around Jacob's office. Everything was spotless already. Aside from emptying the trash, her work would go unnoticed. She was used to it, but her mother always taught her to be thorough.

There was a yellow notepad on the desk with the words "4 Horsemen" scribbled in red ink at the top. There were some things that looked like pigs, or barbecue pits, doodled on the page and some words that appeared to be scratched in haste. Pastor Jacob hated to come back home to a mess of any kind. She decided it was best to put the notepad in the top drawer of the desk for safekeeping and continued to clean.

Felicity emptied the wastebasket next to the desk. Two crumpled white envelopes at the bottom of the basket caught her eye. She recognized her handwriting on the top of one, and pulled it out of the trash. The envelope was addressed to her parents in Juárez and the seal was broken. It was empty. As she processed the situation, the office door flew open.

"I can't believe you let you let that kid live. I always told you, no loose ends," Jacob spoke into his cell phone. "You can be damned sure we're gonna have a talk about that later. Well, 'sorry' ain't gonna do shit for us now, is it? Naldo, bring him here. I don't want to hear it. Just bring him here now. We'll take care of it. Look Naldo, you're, like, less than five minutes away. We'll figure it out when you get here. Go through the side door. Shit, Naldo, I'm getting a call or text or something. I'll talk to you in a minute." Jacob hung up. "Jesus Christ," Jacob said, shaking his head.

"Pastor Jacob," Felicity started.

"Well, hello Felicity. What the hell are you doing here this fine Sunday morning?" Jacob asked.

"Pastor Jacob," Felicity said, "I am cleaning office and I empty la basura and I see you no send out my letters. Why you no do that, Pastor Jacob?"

"Fliss," Jacob said, "I am a bit busy at the moment. We'll talk about this another time. Naldo is on his way here and I'm gonna need you gone, A-sap. Comprendo?"

Felicity shook the envelopes near Pastor Jacob's face and raised her voice. "I give you this por mí familia. Why you no send it?"

"Not now, Felicity. Later," Jacob said.

"Pastor Jacob, please," Felicity persisted. "It's my family. Why would." Felicity's question was interrupted by a quick backhand to her face.

"Jesus Christ, little girl, shut the fuck up for a second," Jacob said. "I got some things going on. I got no time for your bullshit at the moment, you understand? Don't cry,… or…cry. I can't give an actual shit to whatever is going on in your little world right now."

Felicity dropped to her knees. She held her face, crying, as Naldo rushed through the door. A man with his hands zip tied and head covered with a black cloth bag, was pushed through the doorway. He fell onto the floor next to her.

* * *

"SAW WHAT YOU DID BACK IN FRISCO. OTW TO HOUSE. DONT BE THERE!!!!" Jacob read the text just before another text came in. "NEW EVIDENCE 4 CASE DONT BE FOUND WITH PRIEST! BESTT ADVICE!! TTYL." Jacob tried to take it all in. He didn't enjoy texting. So informal and hard to decipher. Was he being yelled at? All the capital letters seemed unnecessary and the abbreviations might as well have been hieroglyphics.

"Naldo, I think we may need to go to a new location," Jacob said. "Grab him, and I'm pretty sure we're gonna need to take her with us, too. You got more ties on you? I got a big production coming up. Shit, Naldo, there is livestock involved. I am not going to disappoint that crowd. Naldo, don't worry my friend, I gotta inside connection. We are at least two steps ahead of the game. We just can't hang around here anymore. Let's get to the church first and then worry what we're gonna do with these two."

"Sir," Naldo said as he zip tied Felicity's hands behind her back. "With all due respect, I'm going to lay low for awhile. Leave town. I suggest you do the same." Felicity screamed and Naldo tucked a rag into her mouth.

"I thought we were a team here, Naldo," Jacob said. "Where would you go?"

Felicity did her best to kick her legs in protest but Naldo held them together with his good hand. "My family has a ranch just outside of Pánuco, Mexico. My cousin is a priest at a small church there. I need to get back to my roots. It's something I feel I must do."

Daniel stirred then coughed from underneath the black bag. Jacob grabbed a trophy from a nearby shelf and hit him hard in the skull. Jacob placed the trophy neatly back on the shelf, making sure the words "4th PLACE, BALLS FORE JESUS EVANGELICAL GOLF TOURNAMENT" would still be visible to any future visitors. Daniel groaned and slumped forward.

"Suit yourself, Naldo," Jacob said. "Let's just get through today. It's going to be an absolutely unforgettable sermon. Trust me." Jacob stopped and pulled out his phone. "Hold on just a sec, I need to send something if I can figure this damn thing out."

Jacob typed, "I dont Know what your talking about. But if I did thanks for the heads up. Jacob." Send.

*   *   *

LEWISVILLE, TEXAS

"NO TELLIN' WHAT THEY'RE GONNA find back there at that church," Tony said, as the two sped down the road. "Smelled like rotten meat down in that hole."

"We may have solved two cases at once." Aaron said. "Maybe they were working together. I knew that Jacob guy was going to have something to do with this."

"I think it still might be a little early to jump to conclusions about the pastor," Tony said. "I'm sure he has lots of cars registered to him. Could just be some disgruntled employee who works for him. Maybe the car was stolen. I'm just saying, he's a man of God. Let's give him the benefit of the doubt, you know."

"You must really be taken in by his bullshit every week," Aaron said. "I've seen his picture. Looks like a lawyer and a used car salesman had a baby. I think he's got you fooled."

"Hey, anyone who can bring that many people together every week and give a little hope to people who might not have any left, is alright in my book. Who are we to judge?" Tony said.

"$100 bucks, says this guy lives in a mansion," Aaron said. "He pays no taxes and gets people like you to shell out money every Sunday and everyone leaves thinking they did something good for the world. It's crazy."

"I promise, I don't give that much money," Tony said. "He helps people all over the world. A portion of his book sales goes right to African kids."

"Have you read his books?" Aaron asked.

"No, but I got two in my bathroom."

"Did you see the way those priests were living back there?" Aaron asked. "Two of them sharing a bedroom. Nothing fancy. Trying to help the community, not themselves."

"Yeah, when their not diddling twelve year old boys," Tony said. "I'll take my Jesus from someone who wants to be better himself. Not to mention, your priest there probably has a meat locker full of bodies in his graveyard basement. So, there's that."

"No, you're right," Aaron agreed. "I wash my hands of the whole institution. Can't trust anyone these days."

Tony's phone lit up in the middle console.

* * *

"THANKS FOR THE HEADS UP. Jacob" Aaron read aloud from Tony's phone. "What the hell is this, Tony? Are you tipping this guy off?"

Tony grabbed the phone and put it in his pocket. "It's a guy I know named, Jacob. I told him about a good fishing hole I went to once."

"You've never been fishing in your life. You think I'm an idiot? What's going on, here?"

"Alright, alright, it's the pastor. I was going to tell you, but it wasn't the right time yet. When we got word that we would be investigating Jacob Dryer, I figured maybe I could squeeze a little money out of the guy. I wanted to give it to you to help with Heather's medical bills. It was supposed to be a surprise once I got enough to help out. I know you need all the help you can get right now, buddy."

"That's bullshit, Tony, and you know it," Aaron said. "I bet you told him we were coming to his house. Where's he going to be? Is he leaving the city? The country? Where's he going to be, Tony?"

"You don't think I give a shit about Heather?" Tony yelled back. "And, Scottie, you don't think I care about Scottie? I love that kid like he's my own. I'm his godfather for Christ's sake! I see you out here every day. Sure, you do your job, but you can't even crack a smile 'cause you got so much shit going on in that head of yours."

"Just take us to where he is, Tony. You can make this right."

"I love you like a brother, Aaron," Tony said. "Like a fucking brother. We gotta have each other's backs out here. Put our asses on the line every day. For what? For what? Sure as hell isn't for good pay or insurance and it ain't too good for a marriage neither. We put some guy in jail for stabbing his wife in the face and burning his kids, and where's our ticker tape parade? Nobody's looking out for us. That's why we look out for each other."

"Just take us to where Jacob is, Tony. Do the right thing," Aaron said.

Minutes later, they pulled into the parking lot of the Sowing Seeds Christian Fellowship and were greeted by a skinny security guard in an oversized grey uniform. Tony rolled down his window.

"Ya'll are a little early," the guard said. "First service isn't until 9:00."

"You are doing a great job, …Todd," Tony said after looking at the security boy's name tag. Tony showed Todd his badge. "They called us in to beef up security a bit. Not that you can't handle it, Todd. I know you can, but we hear the service is gonna be a good one. A real doozie. Plus we want to check out the place and get some coffee. You know how we like to do. Am I right, Todd? Hope there's some donuts in there too." Tony faked a hearty laugh. "If there is, I'll send some out to you. How do you like your coffee? We gotta look out for each other, you know what I'm saying, Todd?" Tony shot a quick glance over at Aaron in the passenger seat.

"That would be awesome," Todd said. "They put us out here early, but we don't get a break till after service. I don't really like coffee, but two glazed would be good and a lemonade, if it's not too much trouble."

"You got it, Todd," Tony said. "You keep up the good work, okay?"

"Thank you, sir," Todd said. "Ya'll too."

* * *

TONY AND AARON PULLED INTO a parking space closest to the entrance of the church. The rest of the lot was empty but it wouldn't be long before the whole place was filled with cars.

"Usually, I have to park out in 'BFE'. This is a nice change," Tony said. "VIP treatment and they don't even know it."

"I can't believe you come to this place. Look at the size of it," Aaron said. "This is how people go to church nowadays? Seems ridiculous. You can't pray at home? Let's just get in the door without raising too many eyebrows. We don't want Dreyer to catch wind of us being here. I like the security angle thing you did there. Good call."

"So are we good, Aaron?" Tony asked. "I want things to be good with us."

"We're good," Aaron said. "I'll make sure the report just states the facts. Obstructing justice. You'll get a slap on the wrist and, maybe, a little time off. You could use it. Draeger won't come down too hard on you."

"You're still gonna rat me out?" Tony said. "After all we been through."

"I have to do what's right," Aaron answered. "Everything's going to be okay."

"I'm not so sure about that, buddy," Tony said. "I have a feeling we both might regret that decision."

12

SOWING SEEDS CHRISTIAN FELLOWSHIP

Southlake, Texas

NALDO WAITED FOR THE GARAGE door to open completely before driving the black SUV into the private parking garage underneath the church. The dark tinted windows prevented anyone from seeing in, and nobody else was allowed to park in Jacob's personal garage. The door inside the garage led directly to Jacob's office, and no one had access to his office unless he wanted them to. Naldo grabbed Felicity and took her inside before coming back for the priest.

"Okay, Naldo," Jacob said. "I don't think we can do anything with these folks just yet, if you get what I'm throwing at you. We are probably going to have a shit show after the show, but we don't want them to find anything. I know you got your little pilgrimage to go on, but I would appreciate you helping me take out the trash one last time, so to speak."

"I would never abandon you in your time of need, sir," Naldo said.

"Good to hear, my friend," Jacob said. "I haven't gotten any messages from my connection in a bit, so we might be alright, or we could be screwed. Nobody can get in the office from the outside without the code, so I think we're safe keeping the dynamic duo right here."

"Should I untie, Felicity?" Naldo asked.

"Hell no," Jacob replied. "She knows a lot more than she should right now but she is good people. Keep her tied up. We can always find her mom and dad and do a little pinch and poke to ensure she keeps quiet. I would truly hate to lose her. Plus, if she talks too much to the police she'll be in jail for trespassing in this country without a green card." Jacob looked over at Felicity. "You heard that right, Felicity? It's not like they're just gonna send you back to Mexico, they will make sure you don't see the light of day again. You won't ever see your folks. Remember, we know where they live. It'd be a real shame if anything happened to that pretty little sister of yours."

Felicity let out a defeated sigh through the rag stuffed in her mouth and Jacob interpreted it as compliance. "Good girl, Fliss," Jacob said. "I wouldn't treat you bad. You know that. Please don't make me do anything I don't wanna do. But also, know that I will."

* * *

"JUST A ROUTINE SAFETY CHECK," Tony said to the girl behind the locked glass door. Tony showed her his badge and she held up an index finger as if to say, "Give me one second."

She showed back up at the door minutes later with a slightly older boy wearing a red vest; and with the power of the red vest of authority, he unlocked the door.

"Hello sir, my name is Kevin. Do you mind if I take a closer look at your badges, officers?" Kevin asked. "You'd be surprised how many crazies show up here."

"I wouldn't," Aaron said under his breath.

"We just need to be certain," Kevin continued. "Everything looks good here gentlemen. What exactly can we help you with today?"

"We're just here to do a few routine checks," Tony said. "No big deal. You guys have a huge operation going on here and we just want to make sure everything is up to code. We were brought in by Pastor Jacob, to make sure it's safe for everyone and to evaluate the security. Just like you said, there can be a lot of crazies that show up. You can give the Pastor a call and clear it with him," Tony bluffed, "if it makes you feel better."

"Oh no," Kevin said. "We are not allowed to talk to the Pastor directly, especially not before service. I'm allowed to make decisions like this." Todd pulled his red vest straight. "Please, come in officers and let me know if I can be of any assistance."

"Kevin, you have been so helpful today," Tony said. "We'll be looking all over for hazards and possible unintentional safety breaches. We'll do our best to stay out of the way. I'm gonna make sure the Pastor hears about how gracious you've been."

"Thank you sir," Kevin said, blushing.

The detectives walked through the doorway and continued until they were out of Kevin's earshot.

"Look, let's split up," Aaron said. "You take the left wing and I'll take the right. We don't want to cause a scene here. If we can get a hold of the pastor let's take him in for questioning. We need to find the priest, too, if he's even here and not dead already. We'll hold off on calling for back up. I think if the pastor gets a hint we're here, he'll be on the next flight to South America."

"Got it, partner," Tony said. "Keep me posted if you find out anything, and I'll do the same. Just radio me if you need anything."

Aaron stared into his partner's eyes for a moment before nodding his head once in a quick jerky movement. The two went their separate ways.

Aaron started his trek down the right wing hallway. He was going to need to find his way back stage, behind the scenes, without raising too much suspicion. He would use the "safety inspector" routine, drop Kevin's name if he needed, and he always had his badge to fall back on, as a last resort. They could just arrest the pastor after the sermon, but there was a good chance he had a disappearing act lined up. Tony hadn't helped that situation. If they made a big scene at the sermon in front of all those witnesses and he was innocent, the laws suits would come flying in. Someone would end up losing their job. Cops were a dime a dozen, even honest ones, especially when the media got a chance to twist things around.

Tony slowly made his way down the left wing hallway. He stopped and looked over his shoulder and saw Aaron disappear with the curvature of the hall. Tony pulled out his phone to send a text message.

* * *

"I WANT TO TAKE A look at my boy," Jacob said as he began to pull the black cloth bag from Daniel's head. "I bet he's got my eyes. Does he have my eyes, Naldo?"

"I didn't look, sir," Naldo said.

Daniel was on all fours when the bag was removed. His hands and feet were bound. He squinted as his swollen eyes adjusted to the bright lights of the office. Dried blood covered most of his face.

"Can you clean him up for Christ's sake?" Jacob said. "I want to get a good look at him. See how far the apple fell from the tree." Naldo went to the small bathroom in the corner of the office to wet some paper towels.

"Who are you people?" Daniel growled. "Why have you done this to me? Where is Father Quinn?"

"Hold up," Jacob said, "you don't know who I am? Naldo, get back in here and clean Daniel's face. My boy doesn't recognize me."

Naldo came back with the towels and did his best to wipe the blood from Daniel's face. Daniel moved his head from side to side to avoid the cleaning. Felicity watched silently from her spot on the floor.

"Who are you?" Daniel asked again.

"Listen here, son," Jacob said, "can I call you son? It just feels right given the situation. It's been so long. Too long, I should say. Sorry we never got to play catch. I never got to teach you how to drive stick or buy you a beer when you popped your cherry. Hey, maybe there's still time for that last one, right? My son, the father. It's got a nice ring to it, don't ya think?"

"What are you talking about?" Daniel groaned. "Why am I here? If you have done anything to Father Quinn, you will regret it."

"Son," Jacob began, "I don't think you are in much of a position to make anybody regret anything. I don't know who this Father Quinn fella is, so you can just calm down about that. What I do know is that Naldo here, and we are definitely going to have words about this later Naldo, left some unfinished business in a motel room some time ago. We're gonna take care of that today."

"I don't understand," Daniel said.

"I got a few minutes before I need to get prepared for service," Jacob said. "I guess, I can give you that much."

"Sir," Naldo said, "I don't think that's wise."

"Naldo," Jacob said, "If you did less thinking, we wouldn't be in this little mess, now would we?"

"Very well, sir," Naldo said.

"You see, son," Jacob began, "I met your mama back in the Eighties. I never thought much about her until about right now, but I do recall she was a pretty sweet piece of ass."

Daniel fought against his restraints to no avail.

"Don't get all bent out of shape, boy," Jacob said. "It was a long time ago. She used to work for me, on and off. Lupe was her name,

I believe. She used to come to some of my early sermons back in the day, and clean up after the crowd left. You can't find better help than a 'Mescan' girl. Her and her boyfriend borrowed a little cash from me and couldn't pay up, come collection time. I had to teach that boy a lesson. Your whore mother thought she could persuade me otherwise, by seducing me."

"You're lying," Daniel yelled.

"Easy, boy," Jacob said. "She was real pretty and real persuasive, if you catch my drift. Man, she gave it her all. Ended up staggering out of my office, exhausted. I was so taken by her enthusiasm, I let her boyfriend live. I didn't even try to collect another dime."

"That's probably enough, sir," Naldo said.

"Naldo, if I want any shit outta you, I'll squeeze your head," Jacob said and then returned his focus to Daniel. "You see, son, everything would've been fine, but your mom got a little greedy. I guess she couldn't make ends meet back in El Paso so she decided to come up to Dallas to blackmail me. I'm up here doing my best to spread the word of God, and she thinks it's a good idea to start a scandal. I didn't have time to deal with a money grubbing whore, you understand, so we had to make things go away. That's where Naldo came in."

"Sir," Naldo said.

"Will you shut the fuck up for a second, Naldo?" Jacob said. "So we got rid of the problem," Jacob continued. "We didn't realize there was two problems. I guess Naldo did, but he overlooked one, and here we are. So, my boy, it's really great to finally get to meet you. We could do some sort of DNA test, I guess, to be sure, but you look good-looking enough. I'm convinced."

"I will kill you," Daniel said, looking up at Jacob.

"And in a weird way, I love you too, son," Jacob said. "Look Naldo, he does have my eyes. Holy shit. I'm getting all Cat's in the Cradle over here. Anyway, it's been good to catch up. I kinda wish we had more time."

Jacob's cell phone alerted that a text message had been sent.

"WE R AT THE CHURCH. NO BACKUP CALLED. PARTNER IN RIGHT WING READY TO BLOW WHISTLE. MORE $$$!!!"

"Naldo," Jacob said, "put Fliss in the closet here, and get my boy in the safe. We can't have them conspiring. You're gonna clean this up soon, I'm positive. I have a sermon to prepare for."

* * *

"WHERE ARE YOU, MAN?" JACOB said into his phone. "I can't do this texting anymore. I just left my office and I'm in the west wing."

"Which is the west wing?" Tony asked.

"When you come through the front doors, it's the one to the left."

"Okay good, I'm close," Tony said. "Where should I meet you?"

"There is a break room about halfway down but you have to go through one of the doors marked, 'Employees Only'. It should be the third door on the right. It's still too early to have a security guard there, but doors do open in about 15 minutes, so hurry up."

"See you there," Tony said before hanging up.

"Felicity," Naldo said, lifting her up by the armpits. "I am so sorry to do this to you, but it's in your best interest for the time being." He gently placed her on the floor of the maintenance closet and closed the door.

"You don't have to do this," Daniel said. "He doesn't own you. I know you want to make a fresh start. You're not like him."

Naldo grabbed Daniel by the plastic strip separating his hands and pulled up. The plastic dug deep into Daniel's wrists and he winced. "I don't want to hear it. If it weren't for you, none of this would have happened. I should have gotten rid of you when I got rid of your mother."

Naldo threw Daniel head first into the massive safe and slammed the large iron door.

Naldo's phone vibrated in his pocket.

"So we meet again, Detective Tony," Jacob said from across the break room table as Tony walked into the room. "What ya got for me?"

"I don't think things are looking too good, Pastor," Tony said, "but I am doing my best here. What were you thinking grabbing the priest from the church in one of your vehicles?"

"It was on a whim," Jacob said. "I trusted we had you to figure out the logistics of making that go away. What am I paying you for, anyway?"

"Yeah, about that," Tony said, "the ante has gone up. For the time being, I got my partner roaming the halls of this place looking for you and a priest. If he finds either one of you, he's bringing in half the goddamned metroplex police force to shut this place down. Not to mention, I'm going down with the ship."

"That's unfortunate, Tony," Jacob said. "I know you only had the best intentions. I hate when good cops get bad raps."

"Listen," Tony said, "nobody at headquarters knows too much right now. There is a crime scene unit going over that church in Frisco with a fine toothed comb. I have a feeling shit went down there that will have them busy for months and I'm not talking about what you and your giant buddy did. I can keep them off the scent but it's gonna cost."

"Always about money, huh?" Jacob said. "I feel you. I'm the same way. So I take it we need to get rid of your partner then?"

"If we can find a way to convince him to keep quiet, it would be so much better," Tony said. "I tried talking some sense into him but he's just a guy that doesn't like to bend the rules. His wife's in the hospital and needs a ton of money to get some experimental treatment. She's in a coma. Maybe, we could use that as an angle."

"Tony," Jacob said, "I feel you have mistaken me for someone who likes to give a lot of money to cops. Maybe, we'll just threaten to pull the plug on her life support. Everyone's got a weak spot. Heck, maybe we just do it for fun. Either way, we'll take care of it. In the meantime, just know you will be well compensated for your loyalty. How do we find your partner?"

"He's roaming the other wing, looking for you and a way to get backstage. He's about 6'1", dirty blonde hair, and looks like a cop. Don't hurt him if you can help it. He's a good man."

Jacob dialed his phone. "Naldo, I need you to do me a favor."

* * *

FELICITY SAT IN THE CLOSET, gagged and tied up in the dark. Yesterday, she stood behind a bar muddling mint in a bikini, thinking she was doing her best to make her parents proud. Now, she was realizing what an evil man she had been working for the last few years. She listened closely to what the Pastor said to the priest. She couldn't allow herself to just sit there and wait.

She inched herself around the room on her backside. With her back, she felt a dustpan that was dangling from a hook or nail. Either would suffice. Felicity arched her back and was able to remove the dustpan. She, unnaturally, pulled her arms up behind her and caught the zip tie on the exposed metal. After several minutes of rubbing her hands back and forth, the plastic weakened and she was able to break free.

Felicity grabbed a sturdy shelf and pulled herself to her feet. Her ankles were still bound, but she thought it would be easier to deal with that in the light. Her next objective was to get through the door. There wasn't much room in the closet to get a hopping start so she'd have to search for something heavy to break down the door.

Just in case, she tried the knob first. Naldo had neglected to engage the lock. The closet door opened easily into the bright empty office. Looked like Naldo might get another stern talking to.

* * *

"Sophie, I'm heading backstage now," Jacob said into his walkie-talkie. "I assume everything is in place and the horses have been fed and watered. Have maintenance do one final shit check before I get back there."

"Everything is ready, Pastor Jacob," Sophie said. "Your horse is saddled up and the rest are tied together."

"Thanks Sophie," Jacob said, "and let Diane know she did one heck of a job on the props. Naldo showed me a picture of the skull helmet. That thing might give the kids nightmares for a few weeks. It's all perfect."

"Thank you, sir," Sophie said. "I'll be sure to let Diane know. Remember, we are going to have the thunder and lightening going before we open the curtains. When you hear that, get ready."

"You are wonderful, Sophie," Jacob said. "Oh, and tell the camera guys to avoid the extreme closeups, or use one of them filters. Last week, I looked like a damn Shar-Pei in the playback. Anyway, I'm almost here so I'm going to turn you off now. I need my time to get my thoughts in order. No interruptions, you understand?"

"Same as always, Pastor Jacob. Have a great service."

"It'll be unforgettable, Sophie," Jacob said before shutting off his walkie-talkie.

* * *

IT WAS PITCH BLACK IN the safe. Daniel lay on his stomach with his arms tied behind his back and his ankles bound together. He tried to wiggle free, but his every move seemed to make the plastic ties dig deeper into his wrists. The aches and bruises from the last few hour's periodic beatings only added to the hopelessness of the situation. Two lumps on his head throbbed with their own heartbeats. He would have to just sit in the dark and wait for his captors to return.

A rage welled inside him as he processed the new information. Moments ago, he was in the same room as his father, and his mother's killer. Behind closed eyes, Daniel saw red. His breathing became deeper and more exaggerated. For a moment, he smiled to himself as a new scene played in his mind. Both men were shackled in Daniel's hideaway back at the church. He slit their throats, and as the blood spilled down their chests, he dug his hands into the open wounds and ripped back the skin from their faces. Simultaneously, or individually so the other could watch? Who should be first? Daniel's heart rate was slowing and a soothing calmness washed over him.

Daniel's thoughts were interrupted by the sound of a locking bolt disengaging. They were back. He rolled over and sat up. It was time for him to think clearly. He needed to take advantage of any opportunity that could arise. Daniel was ready to chew off their faces, if it came to that.

The heavy safe door opened slowly. A figure was silhouetted against the bright lights of the office. Daniel squinted to get a better look at what appeared to be a mermaid standing in the doorway. He shook his head and looked again.

"Father, I'm so sorry you had to go through this," an angelic voice said.

"Who are you?" Daniel asked.

"My name is Felicity. I heard what they did to you and your mother, and I had to help. I do not know when they will be back."

"They knew you had the combination and they left you here?" Daniel said.

"It was kind of a lucky guess. Pastor Jacob always uses 35, 27, 27. It's from the Book of Psalms. Something about the prosperity gospel. I will try to find something to cut you free." She hopped away from the doorway, her own ankles still tied together.

"Felicity," Daniel said, "I think I have what we need. Grab the crucifix from around my neck."

Felicity shuffled over to Daniel and removed the crucifix.

"I do not understand," Felicity said.

"Push on the face of Jesus, but be careful. It's sharp."

Felicity did as she was told and was shocked when the blade shot from the bottom of the cross. Her bright white smile beamed across her beautiful face. She quickly cut the plastic from her ankles, then got to work on Daniel's bindings.

"Why are you here, Felicity?" Daniel asked.

"Pastor Jacob, took me from my family in Juárez. I thought it was so I could have a better life but he steals my money. Now I cannot leave because I am not legal to be here. I have no money and nowhere to go. I thought Naldo Ortiz was my friend. Now I fear he will kill me. Especially when they will know that I help you."

"You need to leave here immediately, Felicity," Daniel said. "Go through the garage door if you think the code works for that too. Find your way to Saint Anthony's church in Frisco. Ask for Father Quinn and tell him Father Daniel sent you. He will keep you safe and help you get back to your family." Daniel reached into his pockets and pulled out a 20 dollar bill. "This is all I have so it'll have to do. Take the bus if you can, but don't trust anyone."

"Oh, gracias, Father Daniel," Felicity said as tears formed in her eyes. "Thank you so much."

"Thank you, Felicity. You are Heaven sent. Now go. I am going to look around here and see if I can find anything useful. These two must be stopped. 35, 27, 27, right?"

"Si, Father."

Felicity punched in the code and opened the door from the office to the garage, and walked out. Daniel heard the mechanical garage door open and shut as he looked around the office for something he could use as a weapon. Nothing but pens and pencils in the desk drawers. He propped the door to the safe open with a chair and went in to look around.

There were piles of receipts stacked upon overflowing filing cabinets. Nothing of use, so far. In the back of the safe was a large block covered with a blanket. Daniel went over to investigate. He pulled off the blanket.

On top of a wooden pallet, at least three feet high, lay bundled stacks of crisp $100 dollar bills.

* * *

AARON PEERED INTO ALL THE rooms down the hallway. On the right, were mostly offices and the occasional bathroom. On the left, were the entry ways to get down to the floor seats. He came to the end of the hall and saw a door marked "NO ENTRY

AUTHORIZED PERSONNEL ONLY". He felt he was in the right spot. He opened the door and slipped inside.

He entered into a much narrower hallway with fewer doors. His footsteps echoed despite his efforts to tread lightly. Aaron tiptoed down the hall and came to the first door. "PROP ROOM" was written in magic marker on a piece of white paper that was taped to the door. It seemed as good a place to start as any. Aaron pushed the door open.

The smells of paint and lumber welcomed him in, taking him back to fond memories of his days in high school drama club. Aaron rarely brought it up to anyone these days, but he'd always loved the theater. He combed through the rows of wooden crosses, fluffy sheep, and angel's wings. He ran his fingers over the raised letters on the open pages of an enormous bible. He looked up to see doves and butterflies hanging from the ceiling with fishing line, and smiled.

Aaron dropped to floor as his shin bone shattered from the blow of the steel pipe. He instinctively reached for his gun on his descent but it slipped out of his grasp and slid under a shelf when his chin collided with a size 15 boot on its way upward. A giant man in a black suit loomed over him, grabbed his two-way radio, and ripped it from his shoulder.

"The Pastor would like a word with you after service," the man said.

"Who the hell are you?" Aaron said, blood spewing from his lips.

"Who I am, is not important," the man said.

"Naldo, step away from my partner," a familiar voice said.

Aaron looked up to see Tony standing on the other side of the room. His gun was drawn.

"Oh, thank God, Tony," Aaron said. "My life just flashed before my eyes."

"Get outta here, Naldo," Tony said. "I'll deal with this."

The hulking man walked out of the room carrying his steel pipe. Aaron noticed that Tony never holstered his weapon.

"What's going on here, Tony?" Aaron asked. "What's with the gun?" Aaron did his best to stretch his arm under the shelf to locate his gun, without being too obvious. His fingers could barely touch the grip.

"Don't even try it, Aaron," Tony said. "I just want to talk for a second."

"You don't need to have your gun on me. We can talk. Go ahead and talk."

* * *

"I'M IN TOO DEEP HERE, buddy," Tony began. "Together, we could make things okay, you know? I can't get myself outta this one. You tell the chief about this, I'm screwed. I'm looking at jail time."

"No you won't, Tony," Aaron said. "Just put down the gun and we'll talk about it."

"I'm afraid I can't do that," Tony said. "I told them that maybe we could help Heather out. Get her the surgery if we both cooperated. They said they could always just pull the plug on her life support machine. I don't think we're dealing with good guys here."

"Then let's arrest them," Aaron said. "You and me. We'll be heroes. Call in back up right now. Let's make things right, Tony."

"You think they won't rat me out too? Get them in for questioning and they'll tell them everything. The only way is if I have your cooperation. I got your back, you got mine. Like it's supposed to be. Tell me you got my back, Aaron!"

"Just put the gun down. You don't want to do this. We'll do what's right, together."

There was someone else in the shadows. Aaron saw a figure moving slowly behind Tony. He tried not to shift his gaze.

"I'm so sorry, buddy," Tony said, raising his gun. "I love you."

The priest swung the wooden cross down so hard on the top of Tony's skull his legs buckled and he dropped to the floor. Aaron leaned back and desperately searched for his gun under the shelf. Daniel grabbed the handcuffs from Tony's belt and attached one cuff to Tony and the other to the shelf post. Aaron tickled his gun with his fingers and stretched just far enough to grab it. Daniel pried Tony's gun from his fingers and held it by his side.

"Hold it right there, Daniel," Aaron yelled. His gun was pointed at the priest.

Father Daniel looked back at Aaron and paused for a second. Then turned his back on him and left the room.

Aaron pulled himself across the floor until he reached Tony's unconscious body. He grabbed for Tony's two-way radio. "Dispatch, we need back up at Sowing Seeds Christian Fellowship in Southlake. Two officers down."

* * *

"EASY FELLA. YOU'RE A GOOD boy, aren't you? Yes you are. Yes you are," Jacob said, stroking the nose of the white horse. A sparkly white robe, white crown, and white bow and arrow were laid out for him and placed on the giant hydraulic cross that was currently in the down position and stored that way, since it was used often and far too hard to move. It would be out of sight from the audience. One of the horses seemed restless.

Jacob walked over to the last horse in the lineup. It was the pale green one. The helmet fixed to the top of her head was hideous and terrifying. It was as if the flesh had been peeled from her face and only the skull and fangs remained. The fangs were a nice touch, he had to admit. It was perfect, but the poor thing didn't seem too happy wearing it and she probably wasn't crazy about the dye job either.

"It'll only be a little bit longer. You're doing great," Jacob said to the green horse. "You look all mean and vicious, but I know you're a sweetheart. You're just a big ole softie. You're not jealous of the first horse, are you?" Jacob was used to his jokes falling on deaf ears. The green horse snorted her disapproval. "Everyone's a critic, I guess."

Jacob continued to pet the horses and talk to them when he heard a faint sound in the background, as if a door had opened.

"No one is allowed in here," Jacob called out. "This is my prep time. Hello? Is there anyone here?" He looked around and saw no one. The horses didn't seem spooked. He must have been mistaken.

He walked down the line of horses, patting each one on the back. "You're going to do great out there ya'll. Make me proud. I know you will. Time for me to get…" Jacob's pep talk was cut short by what felt like a mosquito bite to the back of his neck. He lifted his arm to swat it away but it fell limp to his side before reaching its mark.

* * *

THE SPLASH OF WATER FELT refreshing, but the sting of the second slap jarred him awake. Jacob opened his eyes and saw a blurry semblance of his son standing over him. He grinned peacefully and tried to reach out to touch Daniel's face. He wished he could hug him but his outspread arms were restrained by thick rope. He wanted to speak, but his tongue was suppressed by a cord pulled tightly across his face. The corners of his mouth bled where the rope had rubbed them raw. Jacob couldn't move, but the dream was nice, nonetheless.

As reality slowly made its way to the surface, Jacob gradually became aware of his predicament. Every limb was tied down. He could neither move nor scream. He tried to focus his eyes on Daniel.

The sound of thunder resonated throughout the church. Now, nearly fully awake, Jacob jerked in his restraints, eyes opened wide.

Daniel looked down at the pathetic man strapped to the wooden cross and cocked Detective Donolla's Glock 22.

"Forgive me father, for you have sinned."

* * *

THE LIGHTS WENT OUT AND the audience fell silent. The sound of thunder started near the stage and then rumbled to the back of the church auditorium. The crowd collectively followed the sounds from their seats with their heads; looking for the source and then looking at each other with childlike wonder. A deafening thunderbolt crashed overhead accompanied by flashes of artificial lightening. The crowd oohed and aahed.

The curtain opened slowly to darkness and the crowd went silent again with anticipation. The thunder and lightening continued, only quieter now. Then nothing. More than a minute passed. The audience grew restless and started whispering to each other; still not convinced if this was part of the show or if they were witnessing technical difficulties.

Then, from the back of the stage, the giant wooden cross began to rise. The audience applauded and waited to see what would happen next. The lighting was terrible. They could see the cross rising and movement on stage, but this performance seemed flawed. The cross continued to rise.

Almost fully erect, and the audience was even more puzzled by the poorly lighted stage. Where was the choir? Even some more thunder and lightening would have made sense. This felt like rehearsal. The cross finally stopped in its upright position. The audience could see something wiggling at the top, but the whole scene was lackluster, at best.

All the lights came on in the auditorium in an instant. The spectators could finally see what was happening on stage. Four horses stood around the cross. More than 60 feet high, at the top of the cross was Pastor Jacob, arms out, as he had done in sermons past. He wore a maniacal grin stretched unnaturally by a rope pulled tightly across his face. He appeared to be trying to shout, but the sound was muffled. The audience looked confused.

Several security guards and young men and women in red vests rushed the stage from the back. They poured down the aisles and made their way to the front. Still unsure, the audience remained in their seats, many pleased to finally see some action.

A gun shot rang out from behind the stage. People screamed and ducked for cover. Most of the crowd got down on the floor in front of their seats. Some of the security guards took cover and some continued to make their way to the stage. Every red vest hit the deck.

On stage, the horses went wild. The ropes that tethered each animal stretched taut to the top of the cross. For a second, Pastor Jacob lurched forward, red faced and grinning, his neck tendons standing at attention.

Three of the horses ran off into the wings. Pastor Jacob's ribcage ripped open as the ropes attached to his wrists and ankles tightened and pulled him apart in all directions. The first six rows of the audience were sprayed with blood and entrails, rivaling Gallagher's best performance.

The skull faced green horse reared back on its hindquarters, downstage. She leaped off the platform into the audience. With an audible crack, she took the pastor's last remaining limb with her. "Death" found her way to the aisle and galloped with a tattered severed leg in tow. The pastor's leg bounced off the stage behind her, kicking five people in the front row with a well polished Oxford.

Millions of people around the world sat in front of their televisions and computers, wide eyed and open mouthed long after their screens went black.

It was the most epic and unforgettable sermon Pastor Jacob Dreyer would ever give.

* * *

FORT WORTH, TEXAS

The painkillers were kicking in nicely, but the throbbing in his dislocated jaw and the agony from his fractured tibia were impossible to put out of his mind. Aaron asked to be taken to Methodist Hospital when the paramedics showed up at Sowing Seeds. He felt he'd be more comfortable in a familiar setting and he could be close to Heather should anything change with her prognosis. She was scheduled to have her tumor removed in three days.

Chief Draeger was kind enough to visit yesterday and drop off some paperwork. "Take your time, but hurry up," Draeger had said, half jokingly. The manila folder was at least three inches thick. The details of the crime scene investigation at Saint Anthony's Church were horrifying, but some of the photos were so much worse.

26 bodies had been uncovered so far, many too decomposed or mutilated to make a positive identification, just yet. The crime scene unit had excavators, trenchers, and backhoes working around the clock at the old cemetery back in Frisco. The catacombs underneath the mausoleum would most likely produce more bodies. Each room contained a homemade torture device reminiscent

of medieval times. The decaying carcass of Father Doyle Heffernan was found in one of the underground rooms. Two fat rats were nibbling on his rotting remains; one was nestled in a gaping hole in the dead priest's abdomen, apparently napping there between meals. A pair of large glass jars was uncovered in the underground lair. One nearly full of human teeth, the other, brimming with eyeballs. Forensics had their work cut out for them.

A light knock on the door broke Aaron's concentration. Dr. Naidu stood in the doorway of his hospital room and Aaron waved him in.

"You're not my doctor, Doc," Aaron said, suddenly realizing the painkillers may be a little stronger than he had previously thought. An overwhelming feeling of dread crept into his addled mind. Something terrible must have happened to Heather.

"Aaron," Dr. Naidu said, "I need to have a word with you."

"Dr. Naidu, I'm not sure I can handle this right now. To tell you the truth, I'm having a hard time figuring out if I'm even awake. No bad news, please. Please tell me Heather is okay. Please."

"Your, wife's condition has not changed, Aaron," Dr. Naidu said. "Something happened late last night that was very unexpected, indeed."

"Lay it on me doctor," Aaron said.

"A package was dropped off at the front desk last night," Dr. Naidu said. "No one saw who delivered it. The security cameras only picked up a blurry figure dressed in all black. It was so fast. The package only had 'For Heather Rider' written on the front. No return address. Nothing else."

"What was in it?" Aaron asked.

"There was a note that said, 'This is for Heather Rider's experimental surgery. See that she gets it. Anything left over should be donated to the children's oncology ward'. That's all it said."

"So what does all this mean?" Aaron asked.

"The package was filled with money, Aaron," Dr. Naidu said.

"Is there enough in there?"

"There was so much money in there, that Heather's treatment will be taken care of and the children will be able to get new equipment and toys and anything else they need. I have already contacted the two doctors in Dallas and they want to see Heather right away. Aaron, I just need you to sign some papers."

Aaron sat in his hospital bed and started to cry. He sniffed and smiled through his tears. "I need a pen, Doc. Where do I sign?" Dr. Naidu leaned in and gave Aaron a hug before standing up and taking a pen out the pocket of his white coat and handing him a clipboard.

Aaron breezed over the fine print and signed each of the five pages enthusiastically. He didn't think Dr. Naidu would try to take advantage of him. "Here you go. All done," Aaron said.

"One more thing, Aaron," Dr. Naidu said. "This was also in the package." He handed Aaron a small envelope that had 'Aaron Rider' written on the front.

Aaron opened the envelope, pulled out the card, and read it to himself:

Do not be anxious about tomorrow, for tomorrow will be anxious for itself. Let the day's own trouble be sufficient for the day.

-Jesus

* * *

FRISCO, TEXAS

"I CAN'T IMAGINE THE POLICE will be here too much longer, my dear." Father Quinn said. "You're safe. Nothing to worry about. No one will even know you're here. Would you like some tea?"

"I am fine, Father," Felicity said. "Thank you so much for taking me in. You are a very good man."

"We'll raise some money so we can get you back to your family. It shouldn't take long," Father Quinn said. "I know what we can do, we'll have a bake sale and, perhaps, we could raffle off something or another. Edna Fischer has a pumpkin bread that'll make you weep."

There was a knock on the door and before Father Quinn could answer, Sister Sarah pushed her way inside. "You've got some mail, Father," Sister Sarah said. "You have some as well, Felicity." She handed a large yellow envelope to Felicity and placed a box on Father Quinn's lap.

"Nobody should know I'm here Father. I am scared to open it," Felicity said.

"It's like Christmas every day here, my dear. Don't be frightened. I don't hear any ticking. That's a good sign."

Sister Sarah left the room and the two sat there with their packages.

"You first, Felicity," Father Quinn said.

Felicity delicately tore the top of the envelope holding it away from her face. No explosives were detonated, so she looked inside. Something that looked an awful lot like money was at the bottom. She reached in and pulled out a bundled stack of crisp $100 dollar bills. She was speechless. At the bottom of the envelope was a smaller sealed envelope. She pulled it out, broke the seal, and read the note.

Blessed are the merciful, for they will be shown mercy.

-Jesus

"Well, that looks alright," Father Quinn said. "Maybe we'll cancel the bake sale, but if there's time, before you go back home, you'll have to try the pumpkin bread."

Father Quinn sat with a card board box on his lap. "Let's see what's in here, then." He did his best to break the seal on the box and, after a few tries with his thumbnail, he was able to rip the flaps open. He pulled a beautiful, shiny, stainless steel tea kettle out of the box.

"Look what we have here," Father Quinn said. "It's magnificent." He held it up and spun it around to take it all in. His reflection was that of a happy child peering into a funhouse mirror. He opened the lid and saw something at the bottom. There was a stack of crisp $100 dollar bills and a note.

Enjoy the tea. I love you father.

-Chuy

Father Quinn put the note in his top pocket. "I tell you Felicity, it's Christmas everyday."

Their ears perked when they heard the riding lawnmower start. The cemetery was in total disarray at the moment. There were holes being dug and heavy machinery cluttered the grounds, but Adam wanted to do his best to help out. There were flowers to be planted and grave sites to manicure. He wanted to be just like Father Daniel, in every way. It was time he took over. He was fascinated by some of the items the policemen loaded into the back of pick up trucks and hauled away. Some the items looked like homemade gym equipment. He learned that the big black bags had bodies in them from eavesdropping on the grownups. Adam was eager for the police to leave so he could finally get to work.

* * *

FORT WORTH, TEXAS

AARON HAD A BIG DAY ahead of him. He'd been out on medical leave for over a month now and he was growing restless to return. Chief Draeger reminded him that it would be hard to chase down a perp on crutches, so unless he wanted to come in and file papers, he should just stay home and relax.

Aaron sat at the table reading the paper while Scottie poured milk and a colorful children's cereal everywhere except the bowl. Their new golden retriever puppy, Chewy, was enjoying Scottie's carelessness and happily vacuumed every crunchy morsel and puddle off the kitchen floor. Aaron had more important matters to concern himself with today. Besides, everyone seemed happy at the moment. No point crying over it.

Today was the day Aaron was to testify against Tony in court. He had already filled out statements and met with the prosecutors but he could be called to the stand by the defense. It would be difficult to testify against his old partner, but Tony did try to kill him, among other things. They'd been through so much together. Now Tony was looking at 30 years for a long list of offenses including, attempted murder, extortion, and obstruction of justice. After seeing Tony was arrested, a prostitute came forward with a forcible rape allegation for his actions in the parking lot of Melnick's Bar. This wasn't going to be a good day for Tony and yet, Aaron couldn't seem to wipe the smile from his face.

"Come and eat at the table, Scottie," Aaron said. "Grab Chewy. We're going to eat breakfast as a family."

Scottie toddled over to the table with his overflowing bowl of cereal and Chewy followed, tail wagging. Aaron felt hands squeeze his shoulders.

"So tense, Honey. You're going to be great today."

Aaron looked up to see Heather standing behind him in a white robe. A white bandana covered her bald head. She was the most beautiful woman Aaron had ever seen.

* * *

PÁNUCO, VERACRUZ, MEXICO

NALDO HAD BEEN DRIVING FOR hours. Luckily, he had no trouble crossing the border. He was just waved on through in Matamoros. Border patrol didn't find it too unreasonable for a Mexican to come to Mexico and the American side was probably happy to see him leave. The grey convertible Sebring allowed the officers to see he wasn't trying to smuggle anything in his car and he had nothing in his trunk. He wanted a clean start.

He'd had some time to process what happened that Sunday in Southlake. He had spent many years convincing himself he was doing God's work. He had been blind. Naldo got wrapped up in the lifestyle and was easily persuaded by Pastor Jacob's forked silver tongue. He could now finally see that Jacob was wrong. He would never have wished such a horrific fate on anyone, but the pastor probably had it coming. Naldo was spared because God had a plan for him and Naldo would honor Him for the rest of his days.

Making his way down the coastline of Tamaulipas, Naldo felt free. With the wind in his hair and the warmth of the Mexican sun kissing his face, he was happier than he had ever remembered being. He stopped in small towns along the way, sampling tacos from street vendors and buying flowers and fruit from the locals to show his support for his people. He wanted to make a positive impact in the lives of everyone he came across.

As he got closer to his destination, the roads became harder to negotiate. Potholes and debris riddled the streets and, at times, the path would almost disappear completely. Naldo was almost home.

He saw a small stone church in the distance. Logs on cinderblocks separated the property from the dirt road. Two burros were grazing in the field. Naldo drove onto the path leading up to the church and parked next to an old wagon. He had sent a letter weeks ago to let his family know he would be coming. He didn't want to use his cell phone in case it was tracked. Given the remoteness of the village and the questionable efficiency of the postal service in these parts, he figured he'd probably be a big surprise.

Naldo stepped out of the car. Chickens scrambled around his feet before running away. People began pouring out of the church with open arms and smiles on their faces. He didn't recognize anyone. It had been at least 35 years since he had seen any of these people and most of them he had probably never met. He thought he saw a familiar face near the back of the crowd. The man in the black shirt and white collar looked vaguely like his cousin but the years had not been kind.

"Primo," the priest said. "Bienvenidos." The priest made his way to the front of the group with outstretched arms. The two men embraced.

"Padre," Naldo said. "Gracias, buenas tardes." Naldo felt his Spanish was a little rusty. "Habla usted Inglés?"

"I know little," his cousin said. "I do my best."

"Gracias, Padre," Naldo said. "I am so happy to be here and see you again."

"We have a room for you behind the church. I hope you think it suficiente. El baño esta atras. You can clean up and we can eat lunch."

"Primero el baño, then go to confessional before lunch, if that is alright, Padre?" Naldo said. "I need to cleanse my soul."

"Bueno," the priest said. "I will tell el otro padre to wait. He es new here, but his Inglés muy bueno."

Naldo found his way to the toilets and was surprised there was running water and a mirror. He splashed water on his face and fixed his windblown hair before making his way to the church.

Six rows of pews were placed before the altar. A painted picture of the Virgin Mary holding the baby Jesus was hung in the sanctuary behind the altar. Candles were lit. The confessional was more of a shed with two doors, but Naldo wasn't here for opulence; he was here to save his soul.

He stepped into the confessional and sat down. He nearly filled up the entire enclosure with his massive body. Naldo made the sign of the cross. "Bless me, Father, for I have sinned. It has been at least 30 years since my last confession."

Naldo winced and quickly brought his right hand up to his left shoulder. He never saw the bee that stung him but certainly felt the pain from its sting. The walls of the confessional began to swirl in and out of focus. Confused, Naldo sought assistance through the latticed screen. Two piercing blue eyes stared back at him.

"I'd say, you're long overdue."